She certainly was different from the rather gauche innocent who sometimes appeared in his dreams

Bryn had to quell an impulse to exact a sweet revenge on her lovely mouth even as it mocked him.

There was an intriguing dislocation between the Rachel Moore he remembered and the Rachel he'd met today. Now and then a glimpse of the ardent, uncomplicated girl peeked through the cool reserve of the woman, arousing in him a capricious desire to probe deeper and find out just how much she had really changed.

DAPHNE CLAIR lives in subtropical New Zealand with her Dutch-born husband. They have five children. At eight years old she embarked on her first novel, about taming a tiger. This epic never reached a publisher, but metamorphosed male tigers still prowl the pages of her romances, of which she has written more than thirty for Harlequin® and more than sixty all told. Her other writing includes nonfiction, poetry and short stories, and she has won literary prizes in New Zealand and America.

Readers are invited to visit Daphne Clair's Web site at www.daphneclair.com.

THE TIMBER BARON'S VIRGIN BRIDE

DAPHNE CLAIR

~ THE BILLIONAIRE'S CONVENIENT WIFE ~

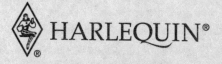

TORONTO • NEW YORK • LONDON
AMSTERDAM • PARIS • SYDNEY • HAMBURG
STOCKHOLM • ATHENS • TOKYO • MILAN • MADRID
PRAGUE • WARSAW • BUDAPEST • AUCKLAND

Recycling programs
for this product may
not exist in your area.

ISBN-13: 978-0-373-52711-3
ISBN-10:   0-373-52711-X

THE TIMBER BARON'S VIRGIN BRIDE

First North American Publication 2009.

Copyright © 2009 by Daphne Clair.

www.eHarlequin.com

Printed in U.S.A.

THE TIMBER BARON'S
VIRGIN BRIDE

CHAPTER ONE

"RACHEL?" BRYN DONOVAN'S grey-green eyes sharpened as he met his mother's cornflower-blue gaze.

Black brows drawing closer together, he sat slightly forward on the dark green velvet of the wing-chair that, like most of the furniture in the room, had been in the family for as long as the big old house. "You don't mean Rachel Moore?"

Pearl, Lady Donovan spread her hands in a surprised gesture. Her slight frame seemed engulfed by the wide chair that matched the one her son occupied on the other side of the brass-screened fireplace.

"Why not?" Her mouth, once a perfect cupid's bow, today painted a muted coral, firmed in a way Bryn knew well. Behind the scarcely lined milk-and-roses complexion and artfully lightened short curls was a keen brain and a will of solid iron.

Bryn said, "Isn't she rather young?"

His mother laughed as only a mother can at a thirty-four-year-old man whose name in New Zealand's business and financial circles engendered almost universal respect. The nay-sayers were mostly competitors jealous of the way he had expanded his family company and increased its already substantial fortunes, or employees who had fallen foul of his rigidly enforced standards. "Bryn," she chided him, "it's ten years since her family left us. Rachel is a highly qualified historian, and I'm sure I told you she's already written a book—in fact, two, I think."

He could hardly tell her he'd tried to expunge all information about the girl from his mind.

Pearl pressed on. "You know your father always intended to write a family history."

"He talked about it." It had been one of the old man's planned retirement projects, until an apparently harmless penchant for the best wines and liqueurs had wreaked a sudden and fatal revenge.

"Well—" the widow's prettily determined chin lifted "—I want to do this as a memorial to him. I thought you'd be pleased." A suspicious sheen filmed her eyes.

Bryn's reputation as a hard-headed though not unprincipled businessman wasn't proof against this feminine form of assault. His mother had emerged from a year and a half of grieving to at last show real interest in something. Her expression today was less strained and her movements more purposeful than since his father's death.

That Rachel Moore's barely seventeen-year-old face under a halo of soft, unruly dark hair, her trusting brown eyes and shockingly tempting, too-young mouth occasionally entered Bryn's dreams, and left him on waking with a lingering guilt and embarrassment, was his own problem. He couldn't in conscience pour cold water on his mother's new project.

He said, "I thought she was in America." Rachel had gone to the States for postgraduate study after gaining her MA in English and history, and had since been teaching university students there.

"She's back." Pearl looked pleased. "She's taking up a lectureship in Auckland next year, but she needs something to tide her over for six months or so because of the different semesters from America. It's ideal, and so nice that we can get someone who isn't a stranger to do this for us. She can stay here—"

"Here? Aren't her parents—" The former estate manager and his wife, who had helped with housekeeping, had left to go sharemilking in the lush green fields of the Waikato district when their daughter started her university studies there. Bryn had vaguely assumed the only contact with his own family since then had been a yearly exchange of Christmas cards and family news. But his mother had always been an inveterate telephone user.

"She's with them now," Lady Donovan told him, "and ready to start in a week or two. She'll need access to our family records, and I wouldn't let them go out of the house." Her expression became faintly anxious. "Of course it will cost, but surely we can afford—"

"No problem," he assured her, reluctantly conceding a rare defeat. "If she wants the job." With any luck Rachel might turn it down.

Pearl gave him her sweetest smile. "Her mother and I have it all arranged."

Rachel had told herself that in ten years Bryn Donovan would have changed, perhaps lost some of his thick, dark hair, developed a paunch from too many business dinners, his aristocratic nose reddened and broadened by the wine imbibed with those dinners if he took after his father. Not that Sir Malcolm hadn't also worked hard and been generous with the fruits of his labours—his knighthood owed as much to his contribution to the national economy as did his public philanthropy.

But his only son and heir was as good-looking as ever.

As she alighted from the bus in Auckland she immediately spotted him among the dozen or so people waiting to greet other passengers or to climb aboard. As if they recognised a man who required more space than ordinary mortals, he seemed to stand apart from those milling around him.

Jeans hugged his long legs. A casual black knit shirt hardly concealed broad shoulders and a lean torso that showed no sign of flab.

If anything had changed much, it was that his habitual understated self-assurance had morphed into a positively commanding presence. Something fluttered in Rachel's midriff and she hesitated on the bottom step of the bus before stepping onto the pavement.

Bryn's eyes seemed silvery in the afternoon light as he inspected the arrivals. When the sweep of his gaze found her and she started towards him, she saw a flash of surprised recognition.

He didn't move, except that his mouth curved slightly into a controlled smile as he watched her approach, while his eyes appraised her jade-green linen jacket over a white lawn blouse, the matching skirt that skimmed her knees, and the Brazilian plaited leather shoes she'd worn for travelling.

He seemed to approve, giving a slight nod before raising his eyes again to the dark hair she'd tamed into a tight knot, which she hoped gave both an illusion of extra height and a mature, businesslike appearance.

Only when she came to a halt in front of him did she

notice the incipient lines fanning from the corners of his eyes, a faint crease on his forehead.

"Rachel," he said, his voice deeper than she remembered. "You look very…smart."

Meaning, she supposed, she was no longer the hoyden-ish teenager he remembered. "It's been a long time." She was glad her voice sounded crisp and steady, befitting a successful woman. "I've grown up."

"So I see." A spark of masculine interest lit his eyes, and was gone.

Rachel inwardly shivered—not with fear but an emotion even more perturbing. Ten years and he still affected her this way. How stupid was that?

"Your mother…?" she inquired. When Mrs Donovan—Lady Donovan now, Rachel reminded herself—had said on the phone, "But of course we'll pick you up in Auckland… No, you can't struggle onto another bus to Donovan's Falls with your luggage…and a computer, too, I suppose," Rachel hadn't thought "we" meant Bryn.

"She's waiting for us at Rivermeadows," he told her, "with coffee and cakes."

Once they'd collected her luggage and were on their way out of the city in his gleamingly polished BMW, Rachel removed her gaze from the mesmeric, sun-sequined blue of the Waitemata harbour's upper reaches alongside the motorway and said, "Thank you for picking me up. I hope it hasn't inconvenienced you."

"Not at all," he replied with smooth politeness.

"But you don't live at home—I mean, at Rivermeadows now, do you?" she queried, keeping anxiety from her voice. Hadn't her mother said something about Pearl "rattling around alone in that huge house"?

"I have an apartment in the city," he confirmed. "But since my father died I've been spending most weekends with my mother, and occasionally staying during the week. I suggested she move out of the place, but she seems attached to it."

The Donovan estate had once been the centrepiece of a small, scattered rural community, but even before Rachel and her family left, it had become an island of green amongst creeping suburbia, not far from a busy motorway.

"It's only half an hour or so from the city," Rachel reminded him. "Does your mother still drive?" She recalled Pearl Donovan had adored her sporty little cherry-red car, sometimes driving in a manner that caused her husband and son to remonstrate, at which she only laughed, saying they had the common male prejudice about women drivers.

A frown appeared between Bryn's brows. "She's hardly left the house since my father died." He paused, then said with a sort of absentminded reluctance in his tone, "Maybe having you there will be good for her."

If he wasn't overjoyed, it wouldn't have been Rachel's preferred choice, either. When her own mother, so pleased with herself, said she'd found the perfect temporary job for her newly arrived daughter, Rachel had to hide dismay on discovering it was at Rivermeadows.

She'd covered it by saying, "It's…um…so far away from you and Dad." To which her mother replied logically that it wasn't nearly as far as America.

Unable to find a more convincing excuse, especially as the hourly rate was way beyond what she could expect from any other temporary position, Rachel saw no choice but to accept. She didn't intend to sponge on her parents for months.

Hoping she'd mistaken Bryn's decidedly unenthusiastic tone, she said, "I'm looking forward to seeing Rivermeadows again. I have some wonderful memories of it."

He cast an unreadable glance at her that lingered for a tiny moment before he switched his attention back to the road.

Rachel turned to look out of the window, trying not to think about one particular memory, having sensibly persuaded herself that he'd have forgotten the incident entirely. It might have been a defining moment in her young life, but while she'd been a bedazzled teenager with an overflow of emotion, even back then Bryn was already a man, someone she'd always thought of as one of the grown-ups.

She said, "I was sorry to hear about your father." Risking a quick look at Bryn, whose expression now appeared quite indifferent, she added, "I sent a card to your mother."

He nodded. "His death was hard on her."

The frown reappeared, and Rachel said softly, "You're worried about her."

"It's that obvious?"

About to say, *Only to people who care about you,* she stopped herself. He'd think she was presuming on an old acquaintance, and rightly so. Devoutly she hoped he had never realised how closely she'd watched his every movement or expression for a whole year or more every time he came near.

Since then she'd become a different person, and maybe he had too. At twenty-five he'd been handed full responsibility for a new sector of the Donovan business, Overseas Development. And he'd run with it, done spectacularly well at bringing the Donovan name to the notice of international markets and establishing subsidiaries in several countries. Now he was in charge of the entire company. No wonder he gave the impression of a man who had the world securely in his fist and knew exactly how to wring from it every advantage.

The house was as Rachel remembered it, a beautifully preserved, dormered two-storey mansion of white-painted, Donovan-milled kauri timber, dating from the late nineteenth century. Its upper windows were flanked by dark green shutters, and a rather grand front veranda extended into a pillared portico.

Old oaks and puriris and the magnificent magnolia that bore huge creamy, fragrant cups of blossom, cast their benign shadows over the expansive lawn and gardens, and the half circle of the drive was still edged with lavender and roses.

Bryn stopped the car at the wide brick steps leading to the ornate front door sheltered by the portico. Almost immediately the door opened and Pearl Donovan, wearing a pale lemon, full-skirted dress, stood for a moment, then hurried down the steps. Rachel went to meet her and was enveloped in a warm, scented hug, her cheek kissed.

"How nice to see you!" Lady Donovan stepped back with her hands on Rachel's shoulders to inspect her. "And you've grown so lovely! Isn't she lovely, Bryn? Quite beautiful!"

Bryn, having removed Rachel's luggage from the car, had his hands full, the laptop case slung over one shoulder. "Quite," he said. "Where do I put her stuff?"

"The rose room," his mother told him. "I'll go and put on the kettle now, and when you're settled, Rachel, we'll have coffee on the terrace."

Rachel followed Bryn up the staircase to one of the big, cool bedrooms. The door was ajar and Bryn pushed it wide with his shoulder, strode across the carpet to a carved rimu blanket box at the foot of the double bed covered in dusky-pink brocade, and deposited the suitcase on top of the box, the smaller bag holding her reference books on the floor. "Do you want your laptop on the desk?" he asked. "Although you'll probably be working in the smoking room downstairs."

It was many years, Rachel knew, since anyone had smoked in what was really a private library, but it retained its original name within the family.

She nodded. "Thank you," she said, and Bryn placed the computer on an elegant walnut desk between long windows flanked by looped-back curtains that matched the bed cover.

He looked about at the faded pink cabbage roses that adorned the wallpaper. "I hope you'll be comfortable," he said. Obviously he wouldn't have been.

Rachel laughed, bringing his gaze to her face. His mouth quirked in response, and the skin at the corners of his eyes crinkled a little. "My mother's right," he said. "You have grown up beautiful."

Then he looked away. "Your bathroom's over there." He nodded to a door on one side of the room. "You'll have it to yourself. If you don't find everything you need, I'm sure my mother will provide it. I'll see you downstairs."

He crossed to the door, hesitated a moment and turned. "Welcome back, Rachel."

She heard his soft footfalls on the hall runner, then on the stairs, still muffled but faster, as though he were hurrying away from her.

After freshening up and exchanging her shoes for cool, flat-heeled sandals, Rachel went downstairs and crossed the big dining room to the French windows that led onto the brick-paved terrace.

Bryn and his mother were sitting at a glass-topped cane table. A large tray held cups and saucers and a china coffee pot with matching milk and sugar containers.

Bryn got up immediately and pulled out another cushioned cane chair for Rachel. The grapevine overhead on its beamed support shadowed his face, and dappled his mother's dress.

While Lady Donovan poured coffee and talked, he sat back in his chair, looking from her to Rachel with lazy interest that might have been feigned. There was a vitality about Bryn, a coiled-spring quality that didn't fit easily with leisurely afternoon teas. He curled his hand around his cup as he drank, and his eyes met Rachel's with a hint of amusement as his mother opened a barrage of questions about life in America.

When their cups were empty Rachel offered to help clear up. But Pearl, who had insisted Rachel was old enough now to call her by her given name, shook her head. "I'll deal with these. We haven't brought you here to do housework. Bryn, take Rachel around the garden and show her the changes we've made."

Bryn, already standing, raised an eyebrow at Rachel and when she got up put a hand lightly under her elbow, his fingers warm and strong.

"Who does do the housework?" she asked him as they descended the wide, shallow steps that brought them to ground level. Surely it was too much for one person.

"We have a part-time housekeeper." He dropped his hand as they reached the wide lawn. "She comes in the afternoon three times a week but doesn't work weekends."

They crossed the grass, passing the solar-heated swimming pool that had been retiled in pale blue, refenced with transparent panels and was almost hidden among flowering shrubs. Their feet crunched on a white-shell path winding through shrubs and trees underplanted with bulbs and perennials and creeping groundcovers.

The Donovans had allowed Rachel and her brothers free rein in the garden on condition they didn't damage the flowerbeds. She had loved playing hide-and-seek, stalking imaginary beasts, or climbing the trees, and knew all the hidden places under low-hanging branches or in the forks of the old oaks and puriris.

"The fish have gone," she said as they walked under a sturdy pergola—a recent addition—smothered by twining clematis, into an open space paved in mossy bricks. Two rustic seats invited visitors to admire a bed of roses instead of the goldfish pond she remembered.

"Too much maintenance," Bryn told her, "and mosquitoes loved it."

Wandering in the shade of tall trees, they eventually came to a high brick wall. Where there had once been a gate giving access to the house her family had lived in, an arched niche held baskets of flowering plants.

"You know we leased out the farm and cottage?" Bryn asked her, and she nodded, hiding a smile. Only someone who'd lived in a mansion could have called the estate manager's house a cottage.

The path veered away from the wall towards an almost hidden summerhouse, its tiled roof moss-covered and latticed walls swathed in ivy geranium and bare winter coils of wisteria.

Rachel hoped Bryn hadn't noticed the hitch in her step

before they walked past it. She didn't dare look at him, instead pretending to admire the pink-flowered impatiens lining the other side of the path, until they came to another pergola that a star jasmine had wound about, bearing a few white, fragrant blooms.

Rachel touched a spray, breathing in its scent and setting it trembling.

A lean hand reached past her and snapped the stem.

She looked up as Bryn handed the flowers to her. "Thank you," she said, suddenly breathless. They stood only inches from each other. His eyes were on her face, his expression grave and intent and questioning. She ducked her head to smell the jasmine and, turning to walk on, brushed against him, her breasts in fleeting contact with his chest.

Heat burned her cheeks, and when Bryn caught up with her she kept her gaze on the jasmine, twirling the stalk back and forth in her fingers as they walked.

And because she wasn't looking where she was going, a tree root that had intruded onto the path took her by surprise and she tripped.

Bryn's hands closed on her arms, his breath stirring a strand of hair that had fallen across her forehead. "Are you all right?"

"Yes. Thanks." Her bare toes stung but she didn't look down, giving him what she hoped was a reassuring smile.

He drew back, checked her feet and hissed in a short breath.

"You're bleeding." He released her arms to hunker down, his hand closing about her ankle. "Lean on me," he ordered, lifting her foot to his knee so she had no choice but to put a hand on his shoulder to balance herself.

"I'll bleed all over you," she protested. "It's nothing."

His hand tightening as she tried to withdraw her ankle, he glanced up at her. "Looks painful," he said. "Let's get you back to the house." Standing up, he placed a firm hand under her elbow again. Inside, he steered her to the downstairs bathroom and, ignoring her claim that she could manage on her own, sat her on the wide edge of the deep, old-fashioned bath and found a first-aid kit in a cupboard. He let her wash her injured foot, then patted it dry with a towel, dabbed on disinfectant and wrapped a toe plaster around the wound.

"Thank you," she said, picking up her discarded sandal and standing as he put away the first-aid box. She'd dropped the jasmine on the counter next to the washbasin and he picked it up as he turned to her again.

Instead of handing it to her he tucked the stalk into the knot of hair on top of her head, gave her an enigmatic little closed-mouth smile, then ushered her out with a light touch at her waist.

Pearl came out from the kitchen, saying, "Are you staying, Bryn? I've got a nice bit of pork in the oven."

He checked his watch. "For dinner, thanks. But I'll be off after that."

Noticing the sandal in Rachel's hand, and the dressing on her toe, Pearl said, "Oh! Are you hurt?"

"Just a stubbed toe," Rachel said, and after assuring his mother she was fine, left Bryn to explain while she went upstairs to unpack.

When she came down again he and Pearl were in what the family called the "little sitting room", as opposed to the much larger front room suited to formal entertaining.

Bryn held a glass of something with ice, and Pearl was sipping sherry. Bryn rose and offered Rachel his wing-backed chair, but she shook her head and sat on the small, ornate sofa that with the chairs completed a U shape in front of the brass-screened grate.

"A drink?" Bryn said, still on his feet. "I guess you're old enough now."

"Of course she is," Pearl said. To Rachel, she confided, "He still thinks of you as a little girl."

"Not so, Mother," he told her, but his eyes, with a disconcerting gleam in their depths, were surveying Rachel. "Although," he drawled, dropping his gaze to her feet, "the plaster does seem like old times." Transferring his attention back to her face, he teased, "You had a hair-raising sense of adventure as a kid."

Quickly she said, "I've grown out of that. I'd like a gin and bitters if you have it, thanks."

Without further comment, he crossed to the old kauri cabinet that served as a drinks cupboard and disguised a small refrigerator. After making the drink he dropped a half slice of lemon into the glass before presenting it to her.

Pearl asked what Rachel thought of the garden, and when complimented said, "A local man comes once a week to keep it tidy and I potter about with the flowers. We've leased out the farm, so there's only the grounds around the house to look after. Bryn suggested *selling* the place—" she cast him scandalized glance that he received imperturbably "—but I hope to have grandchildren some day, and keep the place in the family. After all, Donovans have lived here since it was built. And owned the land even before that."

"It's a wonderful place for children." Rachel didn't look at Bryn. His older sister had moved to England, was living with another woman and, according to Rachel's mother, had declared she never intended to have children. Obviously Bryn was in no hurry to carry on the family name.

At thirty-four, he still had time and with his looks and his money, probably plenty of choice.

The thought gave her a foolish pang. She wondered if he had a girlfriend, and shook her head impatiently to dislodge the thought.

Bryn said, "Something wrong, Rachel?"

"No. I thought—a moth or something…"

"Maybe some insect you picked up from the garden."

He got up and came near, looking down at her hair. Pearl finished her drink and rose from her chair. "I'll go and check on our dinner."

"Can I help?" Rachel asked. But Bryn was blocking her way.

"No, no!" Pearl said. "You stay here. I have everything under control."

Rachel felt Bryn's touch on her hair. "Can't see any creepy-crawlies," he assured her. "When did you grow your hair long?"

"Ages ago," she told him. "While I was at university." It was easier than trying to find someone who could make something remotely sophisticated of her unruly curls.

Instead of returning to his chair, he sank down on the sofa, resting his arm on the back of it as he half turned to Rachel. "How is the toe?"

"Fine. I told you, it's nothing."

"You always were a tough little thing." His mouth curved. "It's hard to believe you're the same scrawny kid with the mop of hair who used to run about the place in bare feet, half the time with skinned knees or elbows."

"Children grow up."

"Yes. I had noticed before you—" He stopped abruptly, staring moodily at the screened fireplace. His voice altered when he spoke again, sounding a little strained. "What happened, before your family left—I'm sorry if I hurt you, scared you, Rachel. I was…" He raked a hand through his hair and turned to look steadily at her. "I wasn't myself. And that's no excuse. But I do apologise."

Rachel bowed her head. "Not necessary. It wasn't just you."

"You were barely out of high school. I should have—I *did* know better."

"Well," she said, lifting her head and making her voice light and uncaring, "that was a long time ago. I'm sure we'd both forgotten all about it until today." Her gaze skittered away from him as she uttered the words.

One lean finger under her chin brought her to face him again. "Had you? Forgotten?"

In ten years Rachel had acquired some poise. Her smile conveyed both surprise and a hint of amused condescension. "Men *so* like to think they're unforgettable," she said kindly, taking his hand from her chin and laying it on his knee. "Of course it all came back to me when I saw you." She patted his hand before withdrawing hers. "Just as if I were seventeen again, with a schoolgirl crush on an older man." Ignoring the twitch of his brows at that, she shook her head, laughing lightly. "Such a cliché, it's embarrassing."

His jaw tightened. A glint appeared in his eyes as he looked at her searchingly, and for a moment she held her breath, before he gave a short laugh of his own. "All right," he said. "I guess I've got off lightly, at that."

Rachel rather thought she had, too.

At dinner Bryn asked Rachel about her work in America and her research and writing experience.

She realised she was being grilled about her qualifications when he said, "This is a bit different, isn't it? How long do you think you'll need to complete it?"

"I hope to produce a first draft in three or four months," she said. "You have so much raw material, it gives me a head start. I won't have to begin by hunting for all the sources I need."

Bryn looked at Pearl. "Do you know exactly what's there?"

Pearl shook her head. "Supposing we found some old family scandal! Wouldn't that be fun?"

"You may not find it fun if you do," Bryn warned.

His mother looked only slightly quashed. "Oh, don't be stuffy, darling! We don't want some dull list of births, deaths and marriages and profit-and-loss accounts."

Rachel said, "I'm sure there'll be plenty of interesting events to colour the bare facts. By the way, do you have a scanner and printer, or is there someplace I can access one? I don't want to handle old documents more than necessary."

Bryn said, "When do you need it?"

"At a guess, in a few days, when I've had time to see what's here."

"I'll see to it. If you need Internet access, I've set it up in the smoking room because I use it when I'm here."

Bryn left shortly after dinner. He kissed his mother goodbye and said, "Rachel...a word?"

She followed him along the wide, dim passageway to the front door, where he stopped and looked down at her without immediately speaking.

Rachel said, "You needn't worry about the book, really. You—or your mother—are paying for it, and have total control over what goes in, or doesn't."

He smiled faintly. "I'm sure we can trust your discretion, Rachel. It's my mother I'm concerned about. She's always been inclined to go overboard on any new enthusiasm. If she looks like tiring herself out I'd appreciate it if you'd let me know, quietly."

Years ago she'd have blindly agreed to anything Bryn asked of her. But she didn't fancy going behind Pearl's back. "If I see anything to be worried about," she said carefully, "of course I'll do whatever's necessary."

He didn't miss the evasion. "She's not as strong as she likes to pretend."

"If you think she needs a nursemaid—"

Bryn gave a crack of laughter. "She'd skin me alive if I suggested it."

"Hardly." Her tone dry, she let her gaze roam over his tall, strong body before returning to his face.

He watched her, his mouth lifting at one corner, a faint glow in his eyes. "I wasn't suggesting you add nursemaid to your duties. It's good she has someone in the house anyway." He paused. "This scanner-printer. Any particular specifications?"

"A good OCR programme. It needs to read documents." She told him the make and model of her computer. He opened the door, hesitated, then leaned towards her and touched his lips briefly to her cheek. "Good night, Rachel."

After closing the door behind him she stood for a moment, the warmth of his lips fading from her skin, then mentally she shook herself and turned to see Pearl come out of the kitchen at the end of the passageway.

"What did Bryn want?" the older woman asked.

"Oh, it was about the scanner," Rachel said. Then she

added, "And he said he's glad you have someone in the house."

"He worries too much. I love this place, and I intend to stay until they carry me out in a box. Or until Bryn has a family and moves in—should they want to."

"I'm sure he wouldn't want you to leave if he did that."

"His wife might. And I might too by then." Rather wistfully Pearl tacked on, "If it ever happens."

By which time Rachel would be long gone, she told herself. Not that it mattered anyway.

CHAPTER TWO

BRYN DROVE OFF feeling oddly dissatisfied with himself. At least they'd brought that old business into the open, and that should have cleared the air between him and Rachel, as well as easing his conscience. He'd sensed a constraint in her from the moment their eyes met at the bus terminal, and he didn't believe her claim that she'd not given any subsequent thought to their last meeting. A soft, rueful laugh escaped him, remembering the deliberate put-down with which she'd denied it. "Rather overdoing it there, honey," he murmured aloud.

She certainly was different from the rather gauche innocent who sometimes reappeared in his dreams. If she'd never had a similar nocturnal problem he ought to be relieved, but at first he'd felt nothing but chagrin, and had to quell an impulse to exact a sweet revenge on her lovely mouth even as it mocked him.

Instead he'd swallowed the unaccustomed medicine like a man, because she was entitled.

There was an intriguing dislocation between the Rachel Moore he remembered and the Rachel he'd met today. Now and then a glimpse of the ardent, uncomplicated girl peeked through the cool reserve of the woman, arousing in him a capricious desire to probe deeper and find out just how much she had really changed.

A glance at the clock on the dashboard reminded him his departure was later than he'd intended. He'd been seeing a lot of Kinzi Broadbent lately, and he'd half promised to drop in after delivering the historian his mother had hired to Rivermeadows. But he hadn't even thought to call Kinzi.

Already on the motorway, he didn't want to use his mobile phone. For some reason he didn't feel like seeing Kinzi now. Instead he drove home and phoned her from there, saying he'd stayed for dinner with his mother, was tired and wanted an early night. Although she accepted the excuse, her voice was a little clipped as she wished him a good sleep. He'd have to make it up to her.

Three days later Rachel was in the smoking room, sorting through boxes of old letters, diaries and papers and spreading the contents over the big table—made of a single slab of thousand-year-old kauri—that dominated the space.

The door opened and Bryn strode in carrying a large cardboard box. Absorbed in her task, she hadn't heard the car.

"Your scanner," he said. "Where do you want it?"

"On the desk?" She stripped off the gloves she was wearing to handle the fragile old documents and hurried to clear a couple of boxes from the heavy oak desk in a corner of the room where she'd placed her computer. "I didn't expect you to deliver it yourself."

"I wanted to check on my mother."

"She seems fine. Did you see her on your way in?"

He'd taken a paper knife from a drawer and began slitting the tape on the carton. "Yes, busy watering potted plants on the terrace. She's excited about this," he said, nodding towards the documents on the table. "How's it coming along?"

"Deciding what to leave out may be a problem. There's such a wealth of material."

They connected the machine to her laptop and she sat down to test it while Bryn stood leaning against the desk.

A sheet of paper eased out of the printer and they both reached for it, their fingers momentarily tangling. Rachel quickly withdrew her hand and Bryn shot her a quizzical look before picking up the test page and scrutinising it. "Looks good," he said, passing it to her.

"Yes." Rachel kept her eyes on the paper. "Thank you. It'll be a big help."

"Glad to oblige," he answered on a rather dry note.

Looking up, she found him regarding her with what seemed part curiosity and part…vexation? Then he swung away from the desk and strolled to the table, idly studying the papers laid out there, some in plastic sleeves. Carefully turning one to a readable angle, he said, "What's this?"

She went over to stand beside him. "A list of supplies for the old sawmill, with notes. Probably written by your great-great-grandfather." Samuel Donovan had built his first mill on the banks of the nearby falls, using a waterwheel to power it. "You haven't seen it before?"

Bryn shook his head. "I know who's in the old photographs my father got framed and hung in the hallway, they have brass plaques, but I had no idea we'd have original documents in old Sam's handwriting. It's an odd feeling." He studied the bold writing in faded ink. "Intimations of mortality."

"There are letters, too." Rachel pointed out a plastic

envelope holding a paper browning at the edges and along deep, disintegrating creases where it had been folded. "This one is to his wife, before they were married."

"'Dearest one,'" Bryn read aloud, then looked up, slanting a grin at her. "A love letter?"

"It's mostly about his plans to build her a house before their wedding. But he obviously loved her."

His eyes skimmed the page, then he read aloud the last paragraph. "'I am impatient for the day we settle in our own dear home. I hope it will meet with your sweet approval, my dearest. Most sincerely yours, with all my heart, Samuel.'"

Lifting his head, Bryn said, "Quite the sentimentalist, wasn't he? You'd never have thought it from that rather dour portrait we have."

"That was painted when he was middle-aged and successful and a pillar of the community." The man in the portrait had curling mutton-chop whiskers and a forbidding expression. "When this was written—" she touched a finger to the letter "—he was a young man in love, looking forward to bringing home his bride."

"Looks like he's won your heart, too." Bryn was amused.

"I think it's rather touching," Rachel admitted. Bryn would never write something like that, even if he were headlong in love. "There's some wonderful stuff here for a historian. I can't wait to read it all."

He was studying her face, and said, "I remember you had much the same light in your eyes after your dad bought you a pony and you'd had your first-ever ride. You came bursting in at breakfast to tell us all about it."

"And got told off for that," she recalled. Her father had hauled her out of the big house with profuse apologies to his employers. It was then she became conscious of the social gap between the Donovans and her own family, although the Donovans had never emphasised it.

"Do you still ride?" Bryn asked.

"Not for years."

"There's a place not far from here where I keep a hack that I ride when I can. I'm sure they'd find a mount for you if you're interested."

"I'll think about it. But I have a lot to do here."

"Hey," he said, raising a hand and brushing the back of it across her cheek, "you can't work all the time. We hired a historian, not a slave."

She tried not to show her reaction to his casual touch, the absurd little skip of her heart. Her smile was restrained. "I'm certainly not on slave wages. The pay is very generous."

"My mother's convinced you're worth it."

"I am," she said calmly, lifting her chin. She would show him she was worth every cent before she finished this job.

His eyes laughed at her. "You haven't lost your spark. I don't doubt that, Rachel. I trust my mother's judgement."

"I had a feeling that you have definite reservations."

"Nothing to do with your ability."

"Then what…" she began, but was interrupted by his mother coming into the room, offering afternoon tea on the terrace.

"Or actually coffee. Unless you prefer tea, Rachel?"

Rachel said coffee was fine.

A few minutes later over their cups she said, "You really should have the records properly archived and safely stored, in acid-proof envelopes and containers. If you had those I could start doing that as I work."

"Buy whatever you need," Bryn said.

"You won't find anything like that in the village," Pearl

warned. "You'd have to go into the city. I told you, didn't I, there's a car you can use?"

"Yes." It had been one more incentive for Rachel to take this job, not needing to think yet about investing in a car.

Bryn asked her, "You do have a licence?"

"Yes. I need to get used to driving on the left again."

"You'd better go with her," Bryn told his mother, and shortly afterwards said he had to leave. The house seemed colder and emptier when his vital presence was gone.

When Pearl hadn't broached the subject by the end of the week, on Friday Rachel asked if it would be convenient to drive into the city.

"I suppose you don't want to go alone?" Pearl asked.

About to say she'd be quite okay, Rachel recalled Bryn's concern about his mother's reluctance to leave Rivermeadows.

Misconstruing her hesitation, Pearl said in a breathless little rush, "But if you're nervous, of course I'll come."

The garage held a station wagon as well, but the red car that Pearl used to drive had gone, its place taken by a compact sedan.

In the city Pearl directed Rachel to a car park belonging to the Donovan office building, and used a pass card for Rachel to drive the sedan into one of the parking bays.

As they shopped for the things on their list, the older woman seemed ill at ease, sticking close by Rachel's side. After they'd made their major purchases and Rachel suggested they have a coffee and a snack in one of the cafés, Pearl barely paused before agreeing. Waiting for their order to be brought, she looked about with an air of bemusement, as if unused to seeing so many people in one place.

Coffee and the cake seemed to make her a little less

tense. Later, as they stowed their purchases in the car, she paused and looked up at the looming Donovan's Timber building. "Why don't we call in on Bryn while we're here?"

"Won't he be busy?" Rachel wasn't sure how Bryn would feel about being interrupted in business hours.

"We needn't stay long," Pearl said. "Just to say hello."

"I'll wait for you here."

"No!" Pearl insisted. "I'm sure he'll be pleased to see you." Less sure, and wondering if Pearl didn't want to enter the big building alone, Rachel followed her into the marble-floored, wood-panelled lobby.

A silent elevator delivered them to the top floor, where Bryn's secretary, a comfortably rounded middle-aged woman wearing huge, equally round glasses, greeted Pearl with surprised pleasure and ushered them both into his office. Rachel was warmed by the approving glance he sent her after greeting them both and suggesting they sit down in two deep chairs before his rather palatial desk.

"Just for a minute," Pearl said, and proceeded with some animation to tell him about their shopping expedition while Rachel admired their surroundings.

Like the lobby, Bryn's office was wood-panelled, the carpet thick and the furnishings solid and practical but obviously made and finished with expensive care.

The whole building spoke discreetly of prosperity and excellent workmanship—not new but magnificently modernised and maintained without spoiling its original character. While building their little empire from one country sawmill to a huge timber enterprise, and diversifying into paper production and even newspapers, the Donovans hadn't lost sight of their history.

It was fifteen minutes before Pearl declared they mustn't

take any more of Bryn's time. He got up to see them out,
Rachel standing back to let Pearl go first. As she made to
follow, Bryn closed a hand lightly about her arm, murmur-
ing, "Thank you."

Rachel shook her head to indicate she hadn't done
anything, but when he smiled at her she felt a momentary
warm fizz of pleasure before they followed his mother
through the outer office and he pressed the button for the
elevator.

Pearl asked him, "Will we see you this weekend?"

"Not this time, I've made other plans."

"Oh—with Kinzi?" She gave him an arch glance of
inquiry.

"Yes, actually."

Rachel, her gaze fixed on the rapidly changing num-
bers signalling the elevator's rise from the ground floor,
was relieved when a "ding" sounded and the doors whispered open.

Rachel worked most of Saturday, but Pearl insisted she take
Sunday off, adding, "You're welcome to use the car."

"I'll just go for a nice long walk, see what's changed. I
need the exercise." Accustomed to working out at a gym,
she had neglected her physical fitness since coming here.

Much of the farmland she remembered had been cut into
smaller blocks occupied by city workers who hankered
after a country lifestyle or whose daughters fancied a pony.
The village of Donovan Falls, once a huddle of rough huts
about Donovans' long-vanished sawmill, and later a sleepy
enclave of old houses with one general store, had grown
and merged into the surrounding suburb.

The little pioneer church the Donovans and the Moores

had attended sparkled under a fresh coat of paint. And the falls named for Samuel Donovan, who had used the power of the river for his mill, were still there, the focus of several hectares of grass and trees donated to the community by Bryn's father, a memorial plaque commemorating the fact. People picnicked under the trees, and children splashed in the pool below the waterfall.

Watching the mesmerising flow make the ferns at its edges tremble as the sun caught tiny droplets on the leaves, Rachel wondered what Bryn was doing.

Whatever it was, he was doing it with a woman called Kinzi. At first she'd thought—not admitting to *hoped*—that "Kinsey" might be male, but Pearl's knowing, interested expression had dispelled any chance of that.

On the journey home from their trip into the city Rachel had suppressed a persistent curiosity while Pearl hummed a little tune to herself in brief snatches and engaged in only small bites of conversation. Rachel had an irrational idea that she was mentally counting potential grandchildren.

And there was no reason to feel ever so slightly irritated about that.

In the afternoon she caught up with her family and friends by e-mail, and on Monday was glad to get back to sorting through the Donovan records.

Pearl helped where she could, explaining family connections or identifying people in photographs. But she was outside dead-heading plants when the phone rang. Rachel picked up the extension in the smoking room and answered.

"Rachel?" Bryn's deep voice said.

"Yes, your mother's in the garden. I'll call her."

"No, I'll catch up with her later. Everything all right?"

"She's fine and the work is going well."

"Did you have a good weekend?" he asked.

"Yes, thank you."

There was a short, somehow expectant silence. Was he waiting for her to reciprocate and ask how *his* weekend was? The thought hollowed her stomach.

Then he asked, "What did you do?"

Briefly she told him, not supposing he was really interested.

He said, "Next weekend I'll take you riding. Unless you've made other plans."

"I haven't thought about it yet—"

"Good. Sunday, around ten. See you then."

He'd put down the phone before she could refuse. And she didn't really want to.

He must have mentioned the plan to his mother, because after talking to him that night, Pearl told her, "Bryn said you're riding together on Sunday. It'll be nice for him to have a companion. I don't think Kinzi rides at all."

"His girlfriend?" Rachel's voice was suitably casual.

Pearl sighed. "Maybe something will come of it this time. They've been seeing each other for quite a long time."

On Sunday Bryn turned up with a long-legged, green-eyed redhead. Her hair was cut in a short, straight, jagged style that would have cost a modest fortune. A primrose cashmere sweater and skinny jeans hugged a figure that most women would give a whole mouthful of teeth for, and high-heeled ankle-boots brought her near to Bryn's height. A short denim jacket finished the deceptively casual outfit.

Kinzi gave Rachel a dazzling smile on being introduced and announced she was here to keep Pearl company while Bryn and "Rachel, isn't it?" went off to "do your horsy thing". On a rueful note she added, "The only time I got on a horse the brute threw me." She laughed, a surprisingly hearty sound. "I know about getting back on and all that, but I thought, why should I? You don't ride, do you, Lady Donovan?"

Pearl shook her head. "It's kind of you to sit with an old lady, my dear. But not at all necessary. And please, let's dispense with the title."

Rachel had to choke back laughter at the uncharacteristic, almost querulous tone of Pearl's little speech. Meeting Bryn's slightly pained expression, belied by the amused appreciation in his eyes, she knew he hadn't missed it, but Kinzi didn't seem to notice.

Whether his bringing Kinzi along had been her own idea or Bryn's, Rachel was very sure Pearl Donovan didn't, and probably never would, think of herself as an old lady.

Perhaps it was the look she turned on her son that made him say, "Ready, Rachel? We'll get going then."

She had put on jeans and sneakers with a sweatshirt and was relieved to see that he, too, was casually dressed, although he wore riding boots.

In the car she told him, "Did your mother mention she had some visitors this week?"

"She asked them to come?"

"I don't think so. They were passing through, I gather." Pearl had invited Rachel to join them for afternoon tea, but she'd declined, not wanting to intrude. Afterwards Pearl had seemed quite animated, describing the middle-aged couple as old friends and saying what a nice chat they'd had.

They were the first visitors Rachel had seen apart from Kinzi. Pearl certainly wasn't doing as much entertaining as she used to. "I think their name was McGill," she told Bryn.

He nodded. "They used to live in Auckland until they retired to a beach community up north. I don't think she's seen them since the funeral. In fact after the first couple of months hardly anyone visited. She hasn't shown any interest in resuming a social life without Dad."

"Give her time," Rachel murmured.

Bryn didn't look convinced. He wasn't used to standing by and letting things happen at their own pace.

The place he drove to offered trail rides and treks, as well as plenty of rolling, open countryside and stands of dark, mossy native bush.

Bryn's big bay gelding seemed pleased to see him, and the owner supplied a pretty, soft-mouthed little mare for Rachel.

They started out at a sedate walk along a broad trail that wound through thick bush, but later when Rachel had got the feel of her mount, enjoyed a glorious gallop across green paddocks under a cloud-dusted sky, ending on a high knoll that overlooked rolling hills and a distant view of the Pacific.

There they rested the horses and dismounted, removing their helmets to admire sheep-dotted paddocks, blue-green stands of old bush in the folds of the hills, and the deep azure line of the horizon.

A few grey rocks seemed to grow out of the ground before them, and they sat side by side on one with a flat, slightly sloping top. Rachel rested her elbows on her thighs, her chin in her hands. At their feet grasses with plumed seed-heads bent before a sudden breeze that stirred her hair, loosening a few tendrils from their confining knot.

For long minutes neither she nor Bryn spoke. Then Rachel said almost to herself, "I never realised how much I missed New Zealand until I came home."

Bryn leaned forward and broke off one of the grass stalks, smoothing the fluffy seed-head in his fingers. "You don't miss the States?"

"Some things, of course. But my heart is here."

"You'll miss your American friends?"

"Yes."

"A man?"

She knew he'd turned to look at her, but kept her gaze on the view. "No one special. If there had been, I suppose it would have been harder."

Abruptly he said, "Kinzi's been offered a promotion—a job in Australia."

She had to look at him then, but couldn't gauge his thoughts. He was staring at the stalk of grass, twirling it backwards and forwards.

"Is she going to take it?" Rachel supposed some response was expected. "What sort of job? I don't know what she does."

"She hasn't decided." He tossed the grass onto the ground. "She edits a fashion and beauty magazine, and the Australian owners want her to take charge of several of their publications over there. It's a big opportunity for her. I don't want to hold her back."

"Would she let you?"

"Maybe," he said, and stood up, looking towards the blue-hazed horizon, his back to her. "If I asked her to marry me."

With a soundless thud something inside Rachel fell from her chest to her stomach. What was he telling her, and why?

Enough of this conversation. Rachel picked up her helmet from the ground beside her and began walking back to where the horses were cropping the grass. "If that's what you want," she said, "you'd better ask her."

She strapped on the helmet, jerking it tight under her chin, and grabbed the mare's reins. The horse turned its head and whinnied as she put her foot into the stirrup and swung her leg over the saddle, then it danced backwards before she'd found the other stirrup.

Bryn caught at the reins and steadied the mare while Rachel took a firmer hold. "That's your advice?"

She looked down at him, exasperated and oddly angry. "I'm not your auntie," she snapped. "It's up to you. Of course if you want to be noble, you could love and let go." Something stuck in her throat, and she jerked the reins from his hands.

He stepped back, black brows raised, his mouth laughing. Then he strode towards his own horse, vaulting into the saddle.

By the time he set the gelding on the downhill path Rachel's mare was well ahead, but he soon drew level.

When she broke into a gallop, the big gelding easily kept pace, but they slowed to a side-by-side walk on the wide track through the bush.

"I don't make a habit of discussing my...affairs of the heart," Bryn said, a sardonic inflection on the final phrase. "Did I offend you?"

"I'm not offended."

"Could have fooled me," he murmured. And then on a note of curiosity added, "Is it a case of female solidarity? Does that weigh more heavily than an old friendship?"

"You and I were never really friends," she argued. "There was such a difference in our ages."

"Our families were close."

"My family were your family's employees."

He frowned. "Surely you're not a snob, Rachel?"

"I'm just stating a fact."

"Why are you angry with me?" He reached out and brought both horses to a halt, their riders knee-to-knee.

"I'm not angry." A half truth. She was annoyed with herself for caring about Bryn's love-life. Some sort of delayed hangover from a silly teenage infatuation. "Only I can't help you."

"I didn't expect it, just thinking aloud, really."

As if she hadn't even been there. Or was a mere sounding board.

Once she would have been delighted at his confiding in her.

The mare gave a snort and shook her mane. Rachel felt like doing the same. Instead she let the horse break into a canter until they reached the yards and buildings where they'd started out.

Back at Rivermeadows, they found Pearl had prepared a cold lunch and set a table on the terrace.

Bryn said he'd like a short swim first, and although Rachel declined, Kinzi changed into a tiny bikini that showed off her perfect body. Helping Pearl place meats and salads on the table, Rachel could hear the other young woman's giggles and little squeals, and Bryn's laughing voice.

Over lunch Kinzi sparkled, complimenting her hostess on the salad and cold meat loaf, quizzing Rachel on whether she'd enjoyed riding again, and teasing Bryn about his affection for his horse, calling him "my cowboy", which set Rachel's teeth on edge but brought a half grin to Bryn's mouth, that inexplicably made her mad again.

It was a leisurely meal and when the others repaired to the little sitting room Rachel excused herself, went to her room to get a book and then slipped downstairs again and into the garden. There she found a secluded spot under a weeping rimu that brushed the ground, and settled down to read.

She'd been there for some time when low voices, male and female, alerted her that Bryn and Kinzi were strolling nearby. Not wanting to eavesdrop, she scrambled up, closing the book, and got her hair tangled in the sweeping branches of the tree before she escaped its clutching fingers. She was picking narrow leaves and bits of bark out of her hair when the other two appeared round a bend in the path and stopped before her.

Kinzi giggled, then covered her mouth and said, "Sorry, Rachel. What have you been up to?" She stepped forward and plucked a small bunch of lichen and a twig from Rachel's head. "There," she said, dropping them on the ground.

"Thanks," Rachel muttered. She must look a mess.

Bryn was regarding her with a faint smile, the skin about his eyes crinkling as though he too was trying not to laugh.

"I was reading," Rachel said, "but it's getting cool."

Determinedly she stepped forward, and Bryn moved aside. She didn't look back to see them walk on.

Upstairs, she brushed her hair and, leaving it loose, lay on her bed and tried to continue reading, but after a while got up and went to the window that overlooked the back garden, staring at nothing.

After a while she saw Bryn emerge from the trees with Kinzi clinging to his arm.

They stopped under the pergola, Kinzi's face turned up to his as she said something that looked like an urgent plea. Then she slid her arms about his neck and kissed him.

Rachel watched Bryn's hands go to the woman's waist, and Kinzi pressed against him on tiptoe, his dark head bent to hers and their mouths clinging together.

CHAPTER THREE

STEPPING AWAY FROM the window, Rachel drew in a long breath and let it out from pursed lips. Why couldn't Kinzi and Bryn conduct their necking in the privacy of the trees? Or in the little summerhouse…? She unclenched hands she hadn't realised had curled into themselves.

The kiss might be a continuation of other intimacies they'd already shared, she realised bleakly. Even more passionate ones.

Don't think about it.

But she couldn't help it. Couldn't help wondering if Bryn had asked Kinzi to marry him, if that kiss had been the seal on her agreement. She tried to tell herself that if so she would be happy for him—for them both. But all she felt was a leaden foreboding.

Shortly she again heard voices from the terrace. Then silence. They'd moved inside. If they were breaking the news to his mother, she should stay away. It was a family affair.

Later she heard more talk floating up from the entryway, then the sound of the heavy front door echoing as it closed.

She waited twenty minutes before descending the stairs to find Pearl sitting alone on the terrace, and pretended surprise that the other two had left.

"Some time ago," Pearl said tranquilly. "They told me to say goodbye to you."

No hint of anything unusual having happened or an announcement made. Rachel swallowed hard and offered to clear the table.

Rachel spent the following weekend with her parents, a family celebration for her father's birthday. Driving south in the compact but solid car, she wondered what had happened to the dashing red model Bryn's mother used to have.

It was ten days before she saw Bryn again.

Overnight the weather had turned grey and windy with spiteful, spitting showers, and Rachel had foregone the morning jog she'd taken up.

By noon thunder was rumbling intermittently, and the showers had become a heavy, persistent downpour. The lawns about the house were puddled and roof gutters overflowed. The garden looked sodden and woeful, some plants crushed under the force of the wind and rain. Inside, the rooms were gloomy and Rachel had to switch on the lights to read. Pearl's housekeeper phoned to say she wouldn't come in today; there was a severe storm warning on the radio. "They say there might be flooding on the road."

Bryn arrived just before dinner, his hair and his business suit soaked despite the crushed yellow slicker he wore. His hair was flattened, rain droplets streaming from it down his face, and his skin looked taut and cold.

"I went to the village before coming here," he said. "They're bringing in sandbags in case the river overflows."

Rachel said, "Could it breach the stopbanks?" She was sure they were higher and more solid now than before.

"This promises to be what they call a hundred-year

storm," he told her. "No one knows what could happen. I'm staying here tonight. Someone will phone if the town is threatened and I'm needed to help."

Pearl, who had grown more and more nervous and unhappy throughout the day, looked relieved and said in that case she just had time to make his favourite pudding.

When he'd gone upstairs to change, Rachel set an extra place at the kitchen table where she and his mother usually ate, while Pearl put the kettle on to boil and began delving into cupboards.

Rachel was placing salt and pepper on the table when Pearl turned to her with a steaming pottery mug and said, "Would you take this up to Bryn, please, while I get on with dinner? He needs something hot right now."

Given no choice, Rachel took the cup she was handed, which smelled of lemon and the sprinkling of nutmeg on the surface of the drink. Pearl said, "Lemon juice, honey and rum. It'll do him good." And she turned away again to the counter.

After carrying the cup carefully up the stairs, Rachel tapped on the door of Bryn's room, but there was no reply. He must be still in the shower. Not wanting to encounter him emerging from the bathroom, she waited for a short while, and on hearing movement, tapped again.

"Just a moment," his deep voice called, then seconds later he added, "Okay."

She opened the door, stepped into the room and saw he was barefoot and had pulled on a pair of trousers, but the top fastening and belt hung undone, while a dry shirt lay on the navy-blue woven cotton covering the big bed beside him. His torso was bare and he was rubbing a towel over his hair.

Rachel stopped dead, struck anew by the male vitality

that emanated from him. Bryn in a suit or a T-shirt and jeans was stunning. Bryn only half-dressed was positively swoon-worthy.

The towel in his hand stilled; in fact his whole body froze for a millisecond, as if he were posing for a Greek statue—he certainly had the physique for it.

"Rachel!" he said, his voice low and vibrant. He hadn't turned on the light but a flicker of lightning whitened the window and briefly illuminated his face, his eyes reflecting silvery fire. The thunder that followed was a menacing rumble, still far away.

One final swipe at his hair left it standing in spikes, and he dropped the towel about his shoulders and roughly combed his fingers through the damp strands.

"Your mother asked me to bring this," Rachel said, determined to act as if the sight of him hadn't sent a bolt of invisible electricity right through her body. "Where do you want me to put it?"

"On the—" His head jerked towards the bedside table, but as she moved forward he scowled, put out a hand and said, "Give it to me. She had no right to do that. You're not a damned servant."

"I don't mind," she said as he turned to put the mug down himself. Knowing how Pearl treasured the furniture, she asked, "Shouldn't you put something under it?"

He sent her a glance, still frowning, and opened a drawer and removed a folded handkerchief to slide under the mug. "Thanks, but I'll have a word with her—"

"No," Rachel said. "Don't. Pearl asked a favour as a friend and I was happy to oblige. Leave it alone."

His mouth went tight for a moment before he relaxed, but his eyes still probed. "You're sure?"

"Absolutely sure. I'm quite capable of sticking up for my rights if I need to."

He laughed then, and pulled the towel from his shoulders to toss it on the bed. "You always were."

Automatically her eyes had followed the passage of the towel before returning to Bryn. He was still watching her, and although the window remained unlit she thought she saw something flame again in the depths of his eyes before he picked up the shirt and started shrugging into it.

Rachel realised she was staring, pleasantly mesmerised.

As she stepped back, about to leave, another flicker of lightning briefly entered the room and a louder clap of thunder made her flinch.

"Are you afraid of storms?" Bryn asked.

"No. Your mother seems nervous. Is that why you came?"

"And because there's a chance of flooding." His fingers were rapidly buttoning the shirt.

As he tucked it into his trousers she said, "I don't remember floods ever coming this far." Once the river had risen and inundated the village on its banks, but the big house hadn't been threatened.

He opened the door of a huge carved wardrobe and pulled on leather moccasin-style boat shoes. "In the nineteen-fifties the house was surrounded by water that came within inches of the front door, according to my father."

"Really? I'll probably come across some reference to it, I suppose."

Bryn picked up a comb, swiped it through his hair and dropped it back on the dressing table. He seemed ready to leave when Rachel reminded him, "Your drink?"

He picked up the mug, sipped from it, then emptied the contents and said, "Right, let's go down."

* * *

Although Bryn expressed appreciation of the chocolate sponge pudding, he seemed rather preoccupied. As the lightning became more frequent and the thunder louder, Pearl shuddered and paled with each rumble, and when they'd finished eating said she was going to bed.

Bryn offered to take her upstairs but she laughed him off. "I don't need my hand held. I'll just hide under the blankets until it's all over."

Rain still pounded on the roof and gurgled along the guttering, and after the dishes were dealt with Bryn said, "Join me for a nightcap, Rachel?"

They went into the sitting room, where Rachel drew the heavy curtains against the rain streaming down the windows, and Bryn poured her a glass of Irish cream, brandy for himself. Although the house had been fitted with central heating Bryn moved the fire screen aside, exposing paper and kindling laid and ready to be lit.

He took a box of matches and touched one to the paper, waited for the kindling to take hold and added some pieces of manuka from a large brass wood-box beside the hearth.

He had just settled back into his chair when the lights abruptly died.

Startled, Rachel said, "Oh!"

"Does it bother you?" The firelight flickered on Bryn's face. "I can get some candles if you like."

"No, it doesn't matter."

"I'll just check the phone, though the fire brigade chief has my cell number."

He left the room and came back, reporting the telephone was working, then sat down again.

There was an odd intimacy in sitting here in the raggedly shifting pool of firelight with the rest of the room in darkness. Afterwards Rachel couldn't remember what they'd talked about, only that they sat there for a long time, that Bryn refilled her glass more than once, and that his rather brooding mood gradually mellowed. While they chatted in a desultory fashion he leaned back in the big chair, his long legs stretched out and ankles crossed, hands cradling a brandy balloon, and his eyes half-closed.

The fire had burned to embers and the French clock on the mantel was showing past midnight when Rachel stifled a yawn and said reluctantly, "I'd better go to bed before I fall asleep right here."

Bryn gave her a lazy smile, stirred from his comfortable position and, with a long-empty glass still in his hand, stood up and took hers. "Wait," he said. "I'll bring some light." The thunder had died and the rain eased a little, but the lights were still off.

He disappeared into the hallway and Rachel sat for a few minutes staring at the glow of the dying fire, then stood up, arching her back and sleepily stretching her arms out and up. Not hearing Bryn's return, when the light from the electric torch he held fell on her she abruptly lowered her arms, feeling self-conscious.

He stopped in the doorway and she walked towards him, the light making her blink, his face hidden behind it as he handed her an old-fashioned Willie Winkle candle holder with a fresh, unlit candle in it and then led her to the stairs.

At the top they trod quietly past his mother's room and stopped at Rachel's door. Bryn followed her inside, saying, "I don't suppose you have matches here."

"No."

He reached past her to put down the torch, then pulled

matches from his pocket, struck one and touched it to the wick, producing a small, flickering flame. As he waved the match out she placed the candle on the dressing table.

In the mirror her head was level with his strong chin, their shoulders almost touching. For a moment their eyes met in that other, reflected world, and as if the candle flame had leapt and flared, something seemed to pass between them.

She turned as he picked up the torch.

"Keep this, too, if you like," he offered.

Rachel shook her head, unable to speak. Surely she'd imagined that moment of electric awareness. A trick of the night, the dancing candle flame and the mirror.

He said, "Good night, Rachel," and she stood holding her breath when he bent towards her and kissed her cheek. He immediately straightened and turned to leave the room.

She was still standing there and he was halfway across the floor when he abruptly stopped, muttered, "Damn it all," and turned back, the light in his hand dazzling her so that she flinched away. He switched it off before putting it down again with a small thunk as he reached her.

In the candlelight he looked big and dark and danger-ous, his mouth set, jaw and cheekbones accentuated, his eyes curiously ablaze.

But his hands were gentle when they framed her face and tipped it upward, and those tightly shut lips were soft when they closed over hers and coaxed her to open them for him.

Her heart was thudding and her hands clenched. She fought the urge to touch him, to wind herself about him and never let go, while her mouth was hopelessly lost in the taste and texture of his, the erotic havoc he was wreaking with lips and tongue and tiny, tender nips of his teeth, not hurting but making her shiver with hot, fierce arousal.

Yet while her body urged her to forget everything but this moment, Bryn and how much she wanted him, her mind remembered Kinzi doing exactly what she herself longed to do, and Bryn reciprocating.

She raised her hands and made herself push against him.

He altered his hold from her head to her waist, bringing her closer even as she pulled back from the kiss.

It was the way he had held Kinzi, kissing her.

Anger came to her aid. She thumped at his chest with her fists, so that he let go abruptly and she stumbled against the dressing table, clutching at the wooden edge while taking a long, ragged breath.

He said, sounding almost dazed, "What is it? What's the matter?"

Starkly accusing, she said, "Kinzi?"

"Kinzi," he repeated, as if he'd never heard the name before. He rubbed a hand over his hair. "I did what you said. She—"

He'd proposed? Her anger ratcheting up several notches, Rachel interrupted him. "Then, what the *hell* are you doing kissing *me*?"

"She's going to Australia."

Rachel's mind whirled like a spinning top. She'd told him to ask Kinzi to marry him if that was what he wanted. Had the woman actually turned him down?

Then she remembered with a ghastly sinking feeling that he'd said he didn't want to hold Kinzi back, and her own flippant paraphrasing of the old saw about letting go the one you love.

A wounded ego or a classic rebound response, even if

he'd only wanted some kind of comfort, any reasonably attractive female might have been the lucky recipient of that kiss she could still feel on her lips, her tongue. She had just happened to be the handiest.

"So," she said, shaken now by white-hot fury, "you thought, well, good old Rachel's available to fill in—"

"I never thought anything of the sort!" Bryn stepped towards her, his eyes fired with temper. "You know me better than that."

"And you don't know me at all," she flashed. "I'm not a little girl or an impressionable teenager any more."

"That's the truth! If you were I wouldn't have—"

His mouth suddenly clamped shut. Then he said, almost muttering the words, "I wasn't really thinking at all. I wanted to kiss you and—" He stopped, then more normally added, "I didn't think you'd object. You took your time."

"I didn't know you were going to do it," she claimed. True, but if she hadn't exactly given him an enthusiastic response, it was also true that she hadn't fought him off at once.

Bryn's head tipped to one side as he regarded her, the anger fading and replaced by an uncomfortably shrewd appraisal. He said, "Is Kinzi your only problem?"

"No." A lot of things contributed to her wariness and her still-simmering anger. Chief among them a suspicion he'd used her as some kind of substitute for his girlfriend. She couldn't help asking, "Did you ask her to marry you?"

It was a moment before he answered. "No."

Which told her nothing really, but she could see from the jut of his chin and the warning look in his eyes that he had no intention of saying any more on the subject. Bryn wasn't the type to kiss and tell. Whatever had passed between him and Kinzi was not for sharing.

Surprising her, he said after a pause, "I won't be seeing her after Friday night. I've promised her a farewell dinner."

And what else? Rachel wondered, then hurriedly hauled her thoughts back from the direction in which they were heading. "I'm sorry it didn't work out for you two," she said, although wondering if Kinzi might be hoping for a last-minute reprieve. "Your mother will be disappointed. She'd like you to get married."

He shrugged. "So would I, in good time."

His gaze turned speculative again, and she shifted uncomfortably, hoping he hadn't thought she was hinting. "Well," she said crisply, "it's late. And the rain's almost stopped. Surely you can go to bed now."

He gave her a wry smile, nodded and said, "Sleep well."

Then he turned and strode to the open door, shutting it firmly behind him.

Rachel stood staring at the solid wood panels for a minute, then began dragging pins from her hair and flinging them onto the dressing table before she remembered the soft patina of its varnished surface, and guiltily moderated her movements, trying to calm the wildly conflicting emotions that wouldn't allow her mind to rest.

Even after she'd put on pyjamas, slipped under the covers and tried to sleep, anger, indignation, confusion and longing mixed chaotically. Her body was alternately hot and melting, then cold and goose-fleshed as her brain ticked over and reminded her that whatever impulse had moved Bryn, it almost certainly had nothing to do with her personally. It was simply a repeat of what had happened before.

Older and considerably more worldly-wise, she wasn't

going to fall into the same trap she'd embraced—literally—as a misguided teenager. This time Bryn was on his own.

Bryn had dropped onto his bed still dressed, except for the moccasins he'd kicked off. Staring into the darkness overhead, he silently cursed himself for all kinds of a fool. He might be a hotshot businessman and have a gift for negotiating deals and being in the right place in the market at the right time, but at the moment his personal life was in tatters.

Kinzi would have needed very little persuasion to stay in New Zealand if he'd presented her with an engagement ring and set a wedding date. In fact that was exactly what he'd contemplated doing until…well, recently. When it came to the crunch he hadn't been able to bring himself to do it.

He'd come to the conclusion soon after hitting thirty that he was never going to find some dream woman.

He'd known several perfectly nice, perfectly suitable and attractive women, and was aware that the older he got the smaller the pool of unattached females became. In his early twenties he'd thought himself headlong in love once or twice, but none of those affairs had turned into a permanent relationship.

He was resigned to never finding the woman of his dreams—actually the only one who appeared in them with any regularity was Rachel, and he'd long ago declared her off-limits. If her brothers had known what took place when she was seventeen—

Quell that train of thought. But as she'd told him tonight so tantalisingly, she was no longer that innocent child-woman he'd so nearly seduced—his forehead broke out in a sweat at the mere memory. He squeezed his eyes shut and flung an arm over them, assailed by familiar guilt.

But now he remembered how tonight her lips had been soft and sweet and accepting of his kiss. A kiss he hadn't meant to take, drawn back to her by the fire-warmed skin of her cheek when he'd touched his lips to it, and the scent of her hair, like fresh summer apples, and her luminous dark eyes in the light from the candle as he'd said goodnight. He could have sworn she was willing him to kiss her.

Damn it, he'd tried to resist, got halfway to the door before his brain surrendered to the urging of his senses, and she hadn't moved, hadn't protested until it was too late, until he'd been drowning in her scent, her luscious mouth, the softness of her hair under his fingers. Until he'd pulled her closer, needing her against him, where he could feel her lovely curves, explore the changes that had filled out her breasts, her hips, brought her to full, ripe womanhood.

Did she kiss you back? his conscience asked sternly.

Maybe not exactly, but neither had she said no when she must have known what he intended. She'd opened her mouth to him, let him do as he willed for all of a minute or two.

She's an employee. He remembered her reminding him that his family had employed hers, as if it mattered.

Maybe it does, to her. Maybe she didn't like to repulse the man who pays her wages. What happened to your rule not to mix business with that particular pleasure? In the office it could be called sexual harassment.

My mother hired her. It's different. Nothing to do with the firm.

He shifted on the bed, dropped his sheltering arm.

Sitting up, he swung his feet to the carpet. He needed a drink.

You've already had a fair bit to drink tonight.

I'm not drunk. Not this time.

He'd never had more than one drink alone since...

Since the last time he'd kissed Rachel Moore. He groaned and headed for the shower, stripped off his clothes and turned on the cold tap, gritting his teeth before stepping under it.

Bryn had left by the time Rachel came down for breakfast.

"He must have gone off very early," Pearl said.

The storm had moved off to the south and was disrupting traffic and flooding small towns, pictures of the devastation forming a large part of that evening's television news. At Rivermeadows the sun reappeared the following day and began to dry up the soaked lawns and gardens.

By Friday, with Pearl's help Rachel had sorted most of the materials she'd been given into roughly date order. On Friday evening she tried to read a historical novel that annoyed her with its minor inaccuracies, while Pearl sat dreamily listening to records and flipping through a magazine.

Pearl looked a little pale and admitted to being tired, having spent the afternoon tying up plants that the storm had battered to the ground, and trimming broken ones while the gardener dealt with fallen tree limbs and shrubs torn up by their roots. For once she hadn't refused Rachel's offer to clean up alone after they'd eaten.

Remembering Bryn's request, Rachel wondered if she should phone him, but this was to be his last evening with Kinzi. The thought wouldn't leave her mind, and after Pearl had opted for an early night, Rachel gave up on her book and went to the smoking room, hoping to absorb herself in work.

After a while she became immersed, and when she heard a car door slam outside and then the sound of a key in the front door, was startled to see the French clock on the smoking room mantel stood at past ten thirty.

Still, surely that was early for Bryn to have left Kinzi. She hadn't expected him to arrive until Saturday.

He pushed open the door she'd left ajar, and said, strolling over to her where she sat at the table, "You're not working at this hour, are you?"

"I'll stop soon," she said, looking up at him. "I had nothing else I wanted to do."

"It's not much of a life for you here," he said. "Is it?" He perched on the edge of the table, so he could examine her face.

"I like it," she said, trying to gauge his mood without being obvious. He looked strong and sexy and his mouth was unsmiling. She thought there were signs of strain about his eyes. "How did your dinner go?"

As soon as the words left her mouth she knew she shouldn't have asked.

His face went wooden, his mouth taut. Then he gave a short, ironic laugh, picked up one of the pens sitting in front of her and tossed it so that it twirled before he deftly caught it. "As well as could be expected," he said. "Very civilized and *triste*."

Sad? Rachel swallowed, watching his hand as he gently replaced the pen on the desk. "You didn't…?" She left the question unfinished. Surely he'd have stayed the night with Kinzi if she'd accepted an eleventh-hour proposal.

But Bryn answered anyway. "No." He got up and strode over to the desk between the long, darkened windows, leaned back on it with folded arms. "She's looking forward to a new job in a new country. She's very excited about it." He paused, looking at Rachel's expression. "What are you thinking?"

"That maybe she's covering up disappointment."

"Kinzi's ambitious. She'll get over it."

"So will you."

"Yes."

His gaze was so steady it was unnerving. She said, "Your mother is rather tired. She's been fixing the storm damage in the garden."

Bryn straightened, black brows drawing together. "I told her to leave it for me and the gardener. That's why we pay these people!"

"She enjoys it, and the gardener was here for the heavy stuff, but I think today she did a bit too much."

He was pacing, hands thrust into his pockets. "If only she'd move—this place is far too big for her."

"She won't do that until—"

He stopped at the other side of the table. "Until she kills herself trying to maintain all this—" He swept an arm in a half circle.

"Your inheritance," Rachel reminded him. Skipping the part about Pearl being carried out in a box, she said, "If you had a family she'd happily move out. That's what she's keeping the place for." As if he didn't know. "It isn't my fault," she added tartly, "so you can stop scowling at me."

"Sorry," he said, but the black brows didn't lift. "Her doctor said—"

When he didn't continue Rachel said, "Does she have a problem?"

Bryn shook his head in an exasperated way. "Blasted man—I've known him for years—wouldn't break patient confidence, but he hinted I should keep an eye on her, and made me swear not to let on he'd said anything. All I could get out of him was she doesn't have cancer or anything immediately life-threatening."

"Then it's probably nothing really terrible," Rachel suggested tentatively.

His mouth twisted. "Ever the little comforter," he said.

Rachel felt her face go still and closed. She stood up and said distantly, "I'm going to bed. Pearl will probably be fine by morning." Then bit her lip because she'd just done it again, offering unwanted comfort.

He caught her before she reached the door, his hand on her arm bringing her round to face him. "I didn't mean to snarl at you," he said. "It's been rather a hell of a day— one of our mill workers had a serious accident, and I'll have to try to explain to the family even though I don't know yet exactly what happened. Tonight I said goodbye to a woman I've grown to…well, that I'd become fond of, and I'm worried about my mother. You just happened to be here when it got on top of me."

Just as she'd happened to be there when he felt like kissing someone, Rachel thought bleakly.

He lifted his other hand and his thumb stroked her cheek, making her insides turn to slush. "Don't look at me that way," he said, "please, Rachel."

She turned her cheek away from his hand. "What way?"

"Like a kitten that's been kicked."

"I *didn't*!" she said, whipping her head back to glare at him.

He laughed, a real laugh of delight. "All right," he said. "A grown-up, very offended cat, ready to spit." He cocked his head to one side, ignoring the childish face she made at him. "A Siamese, maybe…no, they have blue eyes, don't they? Is there a cat that has big chocolate-brown eyes with little gold flecks in them?"

He was examining hers deeply, and she dragged her gaze away with an effort. "I have no idea," she said with determined calm, easing herself out of his hold. "I'll see you in the morning."

Bryn stood in the doorway and watched her mount the stairs, her head high, a small curl lying against the vulnerable curve of her neck, her neat behind moving beneath snug jeans. He leaned against the jamb with folded arms, enjoying the view. After all, if a cat may look at a king….

He'd been called a king of industry. Not a title he particularly relished. It smacked rather of old-time factory owners grinding the faces of the poor into the dust. In these more enlightened times he'd found he got better results from treating his workers well and offering rewards for extra effort. And enforcing safety standards. He hoped today's accident hadn't been caused by slipshod practices.

Frowning, he went to the kitchen to make coffee, then sat there drinking it, his mind going over the day, its ups and downs. Mostly downs. He hadn't been tempted to beg Kinzi to stay. He would remember her with warmth and some regret, but the regret would pass. It always had in the past.

His mother—he suspected her heart might not be all it should be. When he'd first seen Rachel tonight, her head bent so earnestly over some old waybill or business letter, he'd felt the burdens of the day suddenly become lighter. But the news that Pearl had been slaving in the garden and tired herself out brought him back to shouldering his responsibilities.

And he'd hurt Rachel, snapped at her without reason. But she'd never held grudges, and had left him laughing. She had always been able to make him laugh. Until he'd made one of the biggest mistakes of his life, and had no idea how to fix it. She'd had to do that herself. She was strong as well as sympathetic and talented.

He stood up with the coffee cup in his hand and stared out of the kitchen window. A bright moon hung white and aloof over the tops of the trees. He could see nothing but black shadows beneath them, but knew exactly where the summerhouse was. The summerhouse where one dark autumn evening the girl he'd always thought of as the kid next door found him trying to drink himself into oblivion.

CHAPTER FOUR

BACK THEN BRYN had still lived at Rivermeadows, working for the family firm as his father's second-in-command. They'd often talked over business matters there or in the car as they drove to and from the city. The house was big enough for him to have a couple of rooms to himself, and from the age of eighteen he'd come and gone as he pleased.

That night he'd told his parents he was going out with friends, but instead he'd armed himself with a couple of six-packs and a sleeping bag and planned to spend the night in the summerhouse, as he had sometimes with childhood friends or visiting cousins in the school holidays. This time he hadn't wanted company.

So when Rachel unexpectedly turned up, and stifled a small scream on seeing the summerhouse occupied, why hadn't he sent her away immediately, instead of reassuring her, "It's all right, it's only me—Bryn."

She'd seemed to waft like a pale shadow into the small building. For a second, moonlight filtering through the trees outlined her legs under the flimsy, floating white thing she wore—the first time he'd noticed that their childish, sexless contours had become slim ankles, firm and nicely shaped calves, thighs that… He'd stopped there, confounded and confused, and not only by the beer he'd consumed. He didn't remember when he'd last seen her wear a dress.

"Rachel," he said, his voice gruff, "what are you doing here? You should be in bed by now."

She'd laughed, not a little-girl giggle but a low, husky sound that startled him anew. "It isn't that late. I'm not a child, you know."

He didn't know—or hadn't until that moment. Vaguely he recalled she'd had her sixteenth birthday…last year? The age of consent, a voice somewhere deep inside him whispered.

He shoved the thought back where it belonged. He wasn't interested in teenagers. And this was Rachel—he'd known her since she was five years old.

She tripped over the sleeping bag he'd spread on the wooden floor, gracefully righted herself and said, "Are you sleeping here? Why?" Now she seated herself beside him, and pulled her legs up under the white dress, wrapping her arms about them.

"Because I wanted to be alone."

"Oh." The soft syllable expressed disappointment. "I'm sorry, do you want me to go away?"

"No," he said, not knowing what he wanted, but in a slightly befuddled way, unexpectedly glad she was here. "But I should warn you, I'm drinking. Not very good company."

"I wanted to be alone, too," she said, "but I don't mind you being here."

"Good." He reached for another can of beer and pulled off the top. "What's your problem?"

Her shoulders hunched. "Oh, nothing that would interest you."

"Try me." Maybe listening to some teenage storm in a teacup would stop him wallowing in self-pity that alternated with righteous rage.

She stared straight ahead, turning to him a pure young profile. "You know we're leaving soon for the Waikato. Going away."

Bryn nodded. "Are you scared?" Of course, she probably didn't remember any other home but the one belonging to the Rivermeadows estate. He realised he would miss her being around. The tight ache in his gut became tighter. But this wasn't about him. "You'll be okay, make new friends," he assured her, "and you're sure to do all right at university. You're not worried about that, are you?"

"No. A bit nervous." She laid her cheek on her knee as if wondering how far she could trust him. "Only…" Her voice was hushed and shy. "I…I think I'm in love," she said.

Bryn laughed at the irony.

She put her legs down and stood up, ready to flee.

Oh, God, the touchiness of adolescence. He took her hand and pulled her back beside him. "I'm sorry," he said. "I wasn't laughing at you."

"Yes, you were." She was stiff beside him, her head down. But he caught the glitter of tears on her cheek.

"No," he said, hooking a comforting arm about her shoulders. "It's just—well, *snap*! I have the same problem." His voice had turned rueful.

Only slightly relaxing, she surreptitiously wiped her cheeks before turning to him. "Doesn't she love you back?" As if that were unbelievable.

He swilled down some more beer. "I thought she did, but she's sleeping with my best friend." His fist closed about the can and it crackled.

"I'm sorry," she said, sounding forlorn. And quite fiercely she added, "Then she doesn't deserve you!"

"Thanks," he said sourly.

Her voice was soft in the darkness as the moon sailed behind a tree. "Is she very special?"

"I thought so. I wish she'd told me about…him. Or he had. When I found out another way I felt so… Oh, hell!" He threw the empty can out into the bushes, knowing he'd have to retrieve it in the morning.

"Betrayed," Rachel supplied for him. "Can I have some of that?" she asked as he fumbled out another can.

"No," he said automatically. "You're too young."

"Just a sip or two. I'm allowed it at home sometimes. Please?"

She reached for it when he removed the tab, and dubiously he relinquished it, allowing her maybe a third before taking it back, saying sternly, "No more."

"Was this girl your first, um…"

He gave her a hard look and she ducked her head, looking down at her toes, sheathed in pale leather slippers with tiny bows on the front. "I mean," she said, "have you been in love before?"

"Thought I was when I was—" he stopped there for a moment, cleared his throat as he realised "—just about your age. And a couple of times since. This was…I thought this time was different." It had been his first really serious relationship, that he'd thought might last.

Rachel said fervently, "I don't think I'll ever love anyone else!"

This time he forbore laughing, instead saying gently, "We all think that at the time. Does he know?"

She shook her head. "I can't tell him. He's…he wouldn't want to know."

"Why not? You're a beautiful girl, and smart, and fun…"

"Do you think so? *Beautiful*?" She looked up at him eagerly, sounding breathless.

About to say carelessly, *Of course*, Bryn checked himself and looked at her properly. The moon had shifted up in the sky and a shaft of pale light showed him her smooth fore-head, big luminous eyes and a mouth that he realised with a shock was eminently kissable. "Yes," he said, his own mouth suddenly dry. "You are very beautiful, Rachel." She was like one of his mother's perfect, deep-cream dew-kissed roses, with petals just beginning to unfurl.

"Oh!" She breathed it out on a long sigh, her lips parted, her breath feathering his chin. "Thank you, Bryn."

Somehow she seemed to have moved closer, and he became aware of her breast, firm yet tender, against his side.

Breast? Rachel had breasts? Not the little buds he'd sort of noticed she'd started growing when she was…what? Twelve, thirteen—but the real thing!

She's only sixteen, you fool—seventeen? Whatever, she was too young. He eased away from her and grabbed another can to occupy his hands. It was still cold and he wrapped both hands around it as soon as he'd pulled off the tab, thinking he should probably stick it between his legs, where he was uncomfortably hot. But not in front of Rachel. He said, "You'll meet other boys—young men. And one day someone special, when you're old enough." He cleared his throat. "You'd better get back home. Won't your parents miss you?"

"They're out. I told the boys I was going to bed with a

book. They won't go into my room, and I'll be back before Mum and Dad get home."

"Have you done this before?" The beer felt good going down, steadying. He concentrated on the taste of it, the chill. "You shouldn't go wandering around at night on your own. It's not safe."

"I don't wander round. I only come here. It's a good place to think." She wasn't moving, and he was trying to think of a tactful way to send her home when she asked, "Do you think you'll get over…her?"

"I suppose so," he said glumly. At the moment he was too raw to really believe it. "Maybe I wouldn't feel so bad if she'd been cheating on me with someone else. Or if Danny had said something. But it wasn't until I confronted the pair of them, hoping they'd say it wasn't true—"

He stood up, shoving another empty can into the crate. "I didn't mean to go maundering on to you. I was going to get it out of my system on my own."

"I don't mind," she said. Standing, too, she came close to him and put her arms about him, resting her head against his shoulder. "I'm so sorry," she whispered. "I wish I could do something for you, Bryn."

She looked up at him, her eyes sheened with tears—for him! he realised—and her mouth just slightly parted. Her breasts, amazingly full, and hard in the centres, pressed against his chest, and he thought hazily, *No bra.* That thing she was wearing, that made her look like a moonlight nymph, was a nightgown, for God's sake!

He put his hands to her shoulders, ready to push her away, opened his mouth to say something—anything—at the same moment she stood on her toes and touched his lips with hers and breathed sweetness into his mouth.

His body was yelling, "Yes!" His mind squawked a feeble "Oh no," before it stuttered into silence.

And then he lost it completely.

Bryn closed his eyes against the memory, only to abruptly open them again. *Let's not go there.*

He had enough on his plate without reliving that particular episode. Rachel had forgiven—claimed to have forgotten—what had happened that night.

He got up from the bed and impatiently stripped off his clothes, self-prescribing a cold shower that had the desired effect but also brought him wide awake. Tomorrow he'd have to face the family of the injured worker, as well as the government safety inspectors.

The inspection didn't worry him so much, although if they found that the company was somehow at fault it could mean a court case and huge fines. Talking to the family was going to be the worst part. The factory was a three-hour drive away, it was late afternoon and there were no available flights tonight. In any case, the manager had said no one was allowed to see the man yet and he didn't think this was the right time for the CEO to talk with the wife or the man's parents. They were standing by at the hospital, as was the manager.

According to the personnel file Bryn had asked for as soon as he heard the news, the guy and his wife had two young children. The company would make sure they were looked after, but if the father died or remained an invalid for life, there was no way of making up for that.

And dinner with Kinzi had been difficult, preoccupied as he was with wondering if the mill accident had been preventable and whether the man would recover. Kinzi had

smiled too much and spoken in gaily brittle tones of her
new job and finding a place to live in Australia. He'd been
irritated at her manner, and then remorseful, knowing it
was his own mood that caused it.

When he took her home he'd been relieved she didn't
ask him in, instead giving him an eye-to-eye look and
turning her cheek to the kiss he bent to give her before she
said a crisp "Goodbye, Bryn," and stepped inside to close
the door on him.

It didn't make him feel any better that he suspected she
was crying into her pillow right now.

He punched his own pillow and lay back, closing his eyes.
Women.

Kinzi. Would she have stayed if he'd asked? Or would
ambition have won out anyway over the prospect of becoming
his wife and providing heirs for the Donovan dynasty?

His mother. It was no secret she'd like to have grandchildren. She was more anxious than even Bryn's father
had been to see the family name carry on with the family
business. He hadn't told her yet that Kinzi was no longer
a candidate.

Rachel. A smile curved his mouth. Fuming when he'd
compared her to a kicked kitten. All injured dignity when
she went up the stairs, the little-girl curl at her nape reminding him of the unruly child he remembered. She'd had a
temper then, but it never lasted long. Once it was over
she'd be all sunny smiles, her eyes bright and expectant, as
though she knew something good would be just around the
corner. She met life full-on, wholeheartedly, with innocent
openness and confidence in those who cared about her. And
generosity. She'd always been quick to forgive.

People didn't change their essential nature. Underneath

her new grown-up exterior was the Rachel he
known...and in a casual, unthinking way, loved.

Rachel...

He went to sleep with the smile still on his lips.

When Rachel descended the stairs in the morning the smell
of percolating coffee beckoned her to the kitchen.

Bryn was leaning against the kitchen counter, in a white
shirt and dark trousers and sipping from a large cup.
Looking relaxed but ready for action.

He took in her T-shirt, shorts and sneakers with a neutral
glance, and as they exchanged good-mornings he moved
aside for her to pour a coffee for herself. A faint scent of
soap and a hint of aftershave teased her, mingled with the
more pungent aroma of coffee. Almost sure he was looking
at her bent head, she kept her eyes down and sat at the
table. Glancing at the clock, she guessed Pearl would be appearing soon.

"Sleep okay?" Bryn asked, still lounging against the
counter.

"Fine." She took a sip from her cup. "Did you?"

Bryn shrugged, and she said, "You must be worried
about the man who was injured."

"I've phoned the hospital. He's had surgery overnight
and he's stabilised. They hope to shift him from intensive
care sometime today."

"That's good, isn't it?" She wanted to tell him everything would be all right, remove the strain from his taut
cheekbones and jawline. But Bryn wasn't impressed by
well-meaning bromides, as he'd made clear last night.

He didn't even acknowledge her Pollyanna-ism. "I'm
getting on a plane in—" he checked his watch "—a couple

of hours. Maybe I can see him this afternoon. And I have to talk to his family."

He drained his cup, then rinsed it at the sink and placed it on the counter. "I have to go. Tell my mother I'll be back next weekend, will you? It's time you and I went riding again." He gave her a tight little smile on his way out of the kitchen. "And Rachel—sorry I was sore-headed last night."

"Okay." She finished her coffee and followed him to the hallway, where he took a dark jacket from the coat stand before opening the front door for her.

His car sat outside, and they descended the steps together. As Bryn unlocked it and got in, Rachel jogged along the drive, and he slowly passed her, gave her a wave, paused at the gate and accelerated onto the road.

Taking his gaze from the side mirror and Rachel's receding form as she jogged in the other direction, Bryn told himself it would have been more sensible to stay in town last night. Driving to Rivermeadows after dropping off Kinzi had been an impulse he hadn't stopped to analyse.

He'd been keyed up and knew he wouldn't sleep in his apartment, with the muted sound of night-long traffic and the occasional wail of emergency vehicles penetrating the double-glazed windows, and his mind unable to let go of what faced him tomorrow: a hospital visit, a possibly difficult interview with a shocked and worried family, and a meeting with his mill manager and the safety inspectors.

Being with Kinzi had only exacerbated his tension. Not her fault, and Bryn supposed he would miss her, but his only real regret was that he might have given her false expectations.

He'd hoped the drive would help him relax, and that the old house when he reached it would have a calming effect.

But it wasn't until he'd seen Rachel earnestly at work, and she'd turned her big brown eyes on him with a tiny smile curving the corners of her mouth, that he'd began to feel the burdens of the day become lighter.

"What happened to your little red car?" Rachel asked Pearl over lunch.

Pearl looked up from her tomato sandwich. "I sold it years ago. Malcolm wanted me to drive something more 'reliable' as he called it. After I had a teeny little accident, and honestly it wasn't my fault—someone pulled out right in front of me. But he insisted, so in the end I gave in." She sighed. "It didn't stop him having a heart attack though. And since he died…" Her voice trailed off. "I haven't really felt like driving."

"The station wagon…?"

"That was for the farm, really. But after we leased the land I kept it to go to plant nurseries, and collect stuff for things like the annual church fair. Although last year I didn't take part in that…in anything much. Actually I should get some plants to replace the ones we lost in the storm. I suppose the gardener could buy them for me."

"You don't want to go to the nursery yourself?" Rachel queried. And as a flicker of panic crossed Pearl's face, she added quickly, "I could come with you—if that's all right. I can do with a bit of a break."

Pearl said, "But won't you be bored?"

"Of course not. It'll be fun."

"She enjoyed herself," Rachel told Bryn the following weekend as they walked their horses after a good gallop. "We stacked the station wagon with plants, had afternoon tea at the nursery's café. Although she asked me to drive."

"You've been good for her," he said. "I'm grateful to you, Rachel." But she noted the frown on his brow.

"Was she driving before your father died?" she asked.

"Yes, although she complained sometimes that she missed her little red monster. I'm just afraid…" He let the sentence dangle, the frown deepening.

"What?" Rachel asked.

"That she's not driving because the doctor's told her she shouldn't—or she's scared of something happening while she's at the wheel. Maybe a stroke or heart attack."

"Did the doctor hint at anything like that?"

"All he would say was I should keep an eye on her."

Bryn certainly did that. He phoned almost every day. One day the previous week Rachel had answered, and he'd told her the injured worker was on the mend but in for a long rehabilitation. The man had jumped a safety barrier to free a jammed log and got caught in the machinery. He was lucky to have survived. The whole company had been reminded of the strict safety code that operated in all Donovan workplaces, and managers ordered to enforce it to the letter.

"Have you asked her," Rachel said, "if anything's wrong?"

"She said there's nothing to worry about and told me not to fuss." He pushed the gelding into an easy trot as they entered the belt of trees. Rachel let him have a small start before catching up.

When they'd returned the horses and were walking towards Bryn's car he said, "How about we stop for a coffee on the way home? There's a pub along the road with a bistro bar that's not too bad."

Within minutes he drew up outside a country hotel, where dust-covered utility vehicles and smart townies' cars stood side by side in the car park. They sat at a table outside, set on a wide lawn that ended at the riverbank where several people were throwing leftovers to a bevy of ducks and seagulls. On a rock in the middle of the river a grey heron groomed an outstretched wing, its long neck gracefully curved into a half circle.

As she scooped foam from her latté Bryn asked how the book was coming along. He sat back in his chair, a hand curled about his cup of black coffee, a faint smile on his lips and his eyes silvered in the sun. Rachel hadn't seen him so relaxed since she'd arrived at Rivermeadows. In the middle of telling him about a letter she'd found addressed to the first pioneer Donovan by the local Maori chief who had been his landlord, she stopped and said, "I must be boring you."

Bryn shook his head, straightening in his chair to lean his elbows on the small wrought-iron table between them. "I don't remember that you've ever bored me, Rachel." He tipped his head to one side. "I haven't taken as much interest in the family's past as I should."

"Too busy looking after its future?" she guessed. "Although there must be enough money now to keep it going for at least a couple of generations—" She stopped before her tongue ran away with her into *if there are any*.

He looked thoughtful, then shrugged. "That depends on several things."

Like whether he ever has children.

As if she'd summoned it, a child of about four appeared apparently from nowhere. A chubby little boy with olive skin, big blue-grey eyes and cropped fair hair, wearing a T-shirt and jeans.

"Hello," he said, staring at Bryn.

"Hi there," Bryn answered easily. Rachel looked around for the boy's parents, but everyone seemed occupied with their drinks and snacks.

"Have you got a dog?" the child queried, his gaze still fixed on Bryn's face.

"Uh…no, not now. I did when I was a boy, though."

"What was his name?"

"Jet."

"Because he was fast?"

Bryn shook his head. "Because he was black."

The little boy looked puzzled, and Bryn explained, "That's another word for black. What's your name?"

"Toby. I'm going to get a dog when I'm seven. But he'll have to stay at my dad's because my mum doesn't like dogs. I'm going to call him Toa."

"Brave?" Bryn translated the Maori word. "That's a good name."

Toby nodded emphatically. Then he looked up as a man carrying a glass of beer and a soft drink came up to them. "I told you to stay at the table," he said sternly to the boy. And to Bryn, "Sorry, mate."

"No problem," Bryn told him. "We had an interesting conversation."

"You were a long time, Daddy!" Toby explained. "I got bo-ored."

Bryn watched the two of them go off to another table, and Rachel turned her head to follow his gaze. The man put down the drinks and ruffled the boy's hair as he sat down. A cheeky grin lit Toby's face. He obviously adored his father.

When Rachel turned back to Bryn she surprised a strangely pensive expression on his face. Did he envy the other man? Then his eyes returned to her as he said almost defensively, "He's a nice kid. Pity his parents seem to have split up."

"Yes," she agreed, "but his father's still in his life. Some just walk away."

"Some might," he said rather grimly.

Not Bryn, of course. He took his responsibilities seriously. Maybe adding a wife and children to them seemed just too much. She wondered if he'd ever wanted to break away from his family and the Donovan empire as his sister had.

He said, "What are you thinking?"

"Do you like what you do? Your job?" She picked up her coffee cup. "I mean, you didn't really have much choice, did you?"

He sat back as though giving the question some thought. Finally he said, "When I was twelve, thirteen, I desperately wanted to become an astronaut. Like every second boy on the planet." He shook his head. "Otherwise, running the company one day was something I took for granted. And yes, most of the time I like it."

Rachel took another sip from her cup. When she put it down again Bryn reached across the table and wiped a bit of foam from her upper lip with his finger, sending an alarming tingle all the way down her spine.

She used her tongue to remove any further traces, then wished she hadn't as the lazy amusement in his eyes turned to a glint of something much more dangerous. She dropped her gaze to her cup, stirring the remains assiduously.

"Rachel," Bryn said.

Wariness in her eyes, she looked at him. "What?"

He didn't say anything for a moment, then he gave a quiet laugh. "Never mind." A new, probing curiosity in his eyes, he said, "One minute you're the little girl I used to know, the next you're…all grown up."

"I *am* grown up," she reminded him. It wasn't the little girl who had reacted to that casual touch of his finger, it was definitely the adult, sexually aware woman. One who wasn't going to have her head turned by the fact that the great, apparently unattainable object of her foolish adolescent desire had at last actually noticed her new maturity.

Yet she was still haunted by the memory of a night long ago, when for a few ecstatic minutes all her puerile romantic dreams had seemed to be coming true.

Shaking off the memory, and how those dreams had come crashing down on her foolish head, she lifted her cup and drained it, careful that no residue this time would remain on her lips. "Your mother will be expecting us," she said.

The quirked corner of Bryn's mouth and his barely lifted eyebrows told her he recognised a retreat when he saw it. But he didn't comment, instead pushing back his chair and standing. The fact that she stood up too quickly for him to come and move her chair for her was at best a Pyrrhic victory.

CHAPTER FIVE

BACK AT THE HOUSE Bryn suggested a swim. The weather, capriciously, had turned hot and humid despite an overcast sky, and Rachel had planned to shower.

Scarcely hesitating, she said, "Good idea," and went upstairs to get into her swimsuit.

It was low-necked and cut high at the leg, flower-patterned Lycra that she liked for its bold sunset colours, but not nearly as revealing as the tiny bits of cloth Kinzi had worn. When she emerged from her room and ran lightly down the stairs carrying a towel, she was surprised to see Bryn waiting for her below, standing with his legs apart, a towel slung over one bare shoulder, swim shorts low on his hips and showing the muscled strength of his long legs.

For a moment Rachel paused midflight, then slowed her pace of descent to a more decorous one.

Decorous or not, she saw the lazy glimmer in Bryn's eyes as he watched her, taking a leisurely inventory from the top of her head, where she'd tied her hair into a careless knot, to her toes.

She restrained an instinct to hold the towel in front of her, trying to ignore the masculine appreciation in his eyes and her own inevitable response.

Both, the analytical part of her brain reminded her, were natural human reactions with no particular meaning except that we're all wired to continue the species, and an attractive member of the opposite sex stirs primal impulses that civilized people recognise and control.

Rationalising didn't stop her staring at Bryn's near-naked body, or her own from heating, her cheeks from flushing as she neared him.

They walked in silence to the terrace and crossed to the pool. Bryn dived in straight away and Rachel followed. The sunlight at this time of year wasn't strong enough to warm the pool, and the cold water drove everything else from her mind until she surfaced, shaking droplets from her hair.

Bryn had powered away to the end of the pool, and was swimming back. They passed each other midway as she followed his example. A few laps was enough to make her warmer, and they finished eventually at the same end, panting a little.

Rachel turned over and changed to a leisurely backstroke, and Bryn leaned on the pool's edge, watching for a while before he swam after her, more slowly now, catching her up and then keeping pace. "You haven't forgotten how to swim," he commented when they stopped at the other end.

He'd coached her himself, patiently holding her afloat while she practised the strokes she'd been taught at school, hoping to emulate her brother's prowess in the water. He'd shown her how to turn her head to breathe, and to tuck her chin into her chest when she dived so she didn't belly-flop. "It's not something you forget," she said.

Just as she hadn't forgotten anything about Bryn. Memories she'd tried to suppress—and memories that had been buried for years, overlaid by new experiences with the passage of time—kept coming to the surface, tantalizing her and forcing comparisons with the present.

Sex, she thought, had a lot to answer for. Pearl had once been "Mrs. Donovan", a glamorous, kind though distanced figure, but now she and Rachel had established a comfortable adult relationship. Bryn was different. There was no denying the undercurrent of awareness that fizzed between them.

After climbing out of the pool and putting on jeans and a sweatshirt she joined Bryn and his mother on the terrace.

Pearl was saying, "Why don't you take Rachel?"

Bryn looked up as Rachel walked towards them. He rose to pull out a chair for her before reseating himself.

"Take me where?" she asked cautiously.

"The annual Donovan's charity ball," Pearl explained. "Without Malcolm," she said, turning to her son, "I'd only be a spare wheel. And I don't want to go on attending year after year like a ghost at the feast until I'm old and doddery. This is as good a time as any to retire from all that."

"People will miss you," Bryn said, with a slightly stubborn air. "I thought you enjoyed these affairs."

"I enjoyed being with your father," she answered. "Nothing is the same without him."

"I know, but—"

"Don't make me, dear," Pearl said gently. "Please."

Rachel thought he looked momentarily shocked at that. Then he gave his mother a keen, sceptical look. "When," he said, "have I ever made you do anything, my darling mother? I learned long ago not to even try."

She laughed, caught out, and even flushed a little. "Truly, I've had enough of being on my best behaviour for hours on end, trying to remember names and faces and eating too much and dancing with old men who tread on my toes. I wasn't there last year—"

"Everyone understood it was too soon after Dad died."

"Well, I don't want to start fielding condolences again," Pearl said crisply, "and you know that would happen."

"All right." Bryn held up his hands in surrender. "I understand."

Pearl turned to Rachel. "Take pity on him, Rachel. He seems to have somehow lost Kinzi." She cast Bryn a re-proving look as though he'd mislaid the young woman through sheer carelessness. "The ball is in two weeks. You might enjoy it."

Bryn laughed. "After your description?"

His mother's lips pursed but her eyes sparkled at him. "She's young and isn't married to the head of the company." As inspiration obviously struck, she added, "You could in-troduce her to some of the older staff members who might have memories that could go in the book."

To Rachel, she said, "The mayor of Auckland is al-ways there, too, and members of parliament, some people from the arts…"

"I know." Rachel had seen in the Donovan papers the photos of the rich and famous, as well as Donovan employ-ees, who regularly attended one of the social highlights of the year. "I'm afraid it's out of my league."

"Oh, tosh!" Pearl said. "You're as good as any of them, and twice as intelligent as most. Besides being lovely to look at. Bryn would be proud to have you at his side. Wouldn't you, Bryn?"

"Absolutely," he agreed with hardly a hesitation. "But you're bulldozing the girl, Mother. I'm capable of issuing my own invitations, you know. *Will* you take pity on me, Rachel?"

The laughing challenge in his eyes told her the last thing he was in need of was pity.

"Of course!" Pearl told him. "It'll do her good to have a night out. One thing I will say—the music is always excellent."

Rachel protested, "I don't have anything to wear to something like that."

Bryn laughed outright. "The age-old female excuse."

"We'll find you something," Pearl said firmly, and after the briefest pause, added, "Go shopping."

Bryn shot his mother a keen look, the laughter dying from his face. Then he glanced quickly at Rachel as she tried to hide her own surprise. She saw the appeal—almost a demand—in his eyes as he said, "Get something nice, and I'll pay for it."

"You won't!" she shot at him. "I pay for my own clothes."

Pearl said. "Oh, let him, Rachel. Donovan's can afford it. A business expense."

"I can't—" Rachel was certain they couldn't claim that on their tax declaration.

"We can argue about that later," Bryn suggested and said to his mother, "Take her shopping and see what you can do."

"To turn me into a swan?" Rachel asked dryly.

He visibly winced. For effect, she knew. "You know I didn't mean that. You were never an ugly duckling. But as you've pointed out a couple of times—" his eyes gleamed "—you're a woman, aren't you? I haven't yet met one who didn't like to get dressed up occasionally. In fact I seem to remember a pink fairy strutting her stuff around the place for a while…."

Her turn to wince. "I was six years old!" The fairy costume had been a birthday present, her mother's effort to remind her daughter she was a girl, and for a while it was her favourite outfit. But the phase hadn't lasted long. Pink net and gauze wings didn't stand up too well to tree climbing or swinging from tyres strung to a branch. And the wand had broken when she used it as a sword in a play fight with one of her brothers.

She didn't know which was more exasperating, Bryn's frequent reminders of her harum-scarum childhood, or the couple of times he'd shown unequivocally that he saw her as a desirable woman—or at least a stand-in for the one he really wanted.

And here she was again, trapped into taking another woman's place. That the woman was his mother this time didn't much sweeten the pill.

For Pearl's sake she could hardly say no. Offering to take Rachel shopping was another step towards normality for Pearl, a sign that she was ready to break out of the co-coon she'd built around herself after being widowed.

"Well?" Bryn raised his brows.

"All right." Rachel almost glared at him. She was tempted by a sudden notion that she could spend a small fortune and charge it to him in revenge for being manipulated. But to be fair, this was Pearl's idea, and once she'd suggested it he could hardly object without being rude.

If he too felt backed into a corner he didn't show it. "Thank you, Rachel," he said, graciously inclining his head. He sounded so nearly humble she looked at him with suspicion, but he met her gaze with a bland one of his own.

The shopping expedition was an eye-opener for Rachel. Chain stores, no matter how upmarket, didn't even impinge on Lady Donovan's consciousness. She knew by their first names designers whose clientele included American film stars, and celebrities whose names were known across the English-speaking world, and owners of boutiques so exclusive they were almost invisible to the naked eye. In every one of the discreetly sumptuous premises Pearl entered she was immediately recognised and greeted with genuine pleasure.

Rachel tried to assert her independence by declaring she wanted something reasonably priced, but her idea of reasonable seemed at odds with everyone else's.

When one couturier had left them to fetch "something I think will be exactly right for Miss Moore," Rachel murmured in desperation, "Pearl, I really can't spend so much on a dress I'll probably never wear again."

Pearl looked supremely unworried. "You're Bryn's partner for the night and Bryn represents Donovan's. Don't worry about the cost just now. Anyway, you can always sell it afterwards if you like. There's a good market for nearly new designer dresses."

She simply acted deaf to any further attempt at protest, and was obviously relishing her role as fashion mentor. When they eventually settled on a gown Rachel took out her credit card, but Pearl waved it away, saying to the salesperson, "Put it on my account, please."

Rachel knew better than to argue. She'd take it up with Bryn later.

Having inveigled Rachel into new shoes to go with the new dress, Pearl took her to her own hairdresser, who started with a full treatment and then snipped the unruly curls into a lighter, prettier shape.

Pearl also decreed that Rachel should dress for the occasion at Bryn's Auckland apartment, and that Pearl herself would come along—not as a chaperon, but to arrange Rachel's hair for her.

In Bryn's guest bedroom she not only supervised and touched up Rachel's make-up, but also twisted a rope of tiny seed pearls into her hair as she styled it into a Grecian knot, leaving loose curls to frame her face. At the last minute, after Bryn had called that they must leave in five minutes, she took a long leather case from her substantial handbag, and fastened a pearl-and-diamond choker about Rachel's neck.

"Pearl," Rachel said, "I can't wear this!" She had no doubt the gems were the real thing.

"Of course you can. I don't wear it any more—the last thing a woman of my age wants is to draw attention to her neck. And it should be worn. They used to say that you should wear pearls all the time, even in bed, to keep their lustre. It looks wonderful on you, just what that neckline needs."

It would have looked wonderful on anyone. Elegant but not ostentatious, it complemented the satin sheen of the deep gold dress with its intricately pleated bodice showing a hint of cleavage, and the deceptively simple skirt that flared at the hem. "No," Rachel said, "really—"

"Nonsense. It's only a loan, like this." Pearl picked up the incredibly soft, creamy lace wrap that she'd taken from her own wardrobe and dropped it about Rachel's shoulders.

A knock came on the door, and Rachel stood up. Pearl gave her a push towards the door and called, "You can open it."

When Bryn did so, his big form blocking the doorway, in black tie and evening clothes he was more handsome than ever. His eyes darkened as he surveyed Rachel, from the cunningly arranged topknot with pearls peeking from the dark tresses, the jewels that circled her throat and the stunningly designed dress, to the sparkling, high-heeled sandals on her feet.

When the comprehensive gaze returned to her face she saw his jaw tighten, and for a moment feared that he didn't approve.

As he remained silent and unmoving, his mother asked, "Well? What do you think?"

His eyes still on Rachel, he said, "I think she looks… breathtaking."

Rachel said, "Your mother did a good job of the make-over."

"It isn't a makeover!" Pearl scolded. "I just helped enhance your true beauty. Off you go and have fun."

At Pearl's behest Bryn had hired a limo so that Rachel's dress ran no risk of being crushed. The interior was so roomy there was plenty of space between them. Luxurious leather seats and the carpeted floor added to a nervousness Rachel had felt all day. Bryn, sitting with folded arms and appearing oblivious to her, didn't help.

When they arrived the driver pulled up under a pillared portico outside the building, and as Rachel emerged to stand with Bryn on the pavement she was startled by the flash of a camera. After blinking, she forced herself to adopt a slight, composed smile as Bryn's hand on her waist guided her inside.

They were the first to arrive, and Bryn checked with the function manager that everything was going according to plan before other couples and groups began to trickle in. Soon the big room was filled with chattering guests holding glasses of wine and taking canapés from circulating waiters.

Bryn, too, circulated, introducing Rachel to a number of people whose faces she recognised from newspaper photographs or television, and others whose titles or his brief description of their jobs indicated that she would have known their names if she hadn't been out of the country for so long.

"Everyone who's anyone?" she murmured once, as Bryn excused them from one group and moved smoothly across the floor to another.

"Anyone who pays for a ticket," he answered. "Although we make sure that certain people are invited to buy one."

"Certain people" with money or a high profile or more likely both, Rachel deduced as she smiled at a government minister who held her outstretched hand for too long and bent so close she could smell his whisky-laden breath.

Somehow Bryn managed to unobtrusively shift his body so that when the man at last released her hand, his only choice was to face Bryn rather than her, leaving her free to exchange small talk with the MP's wife, a thin, rabbity woman wearing a bright orange dress and too much jewellery.

Other guests, too, glittered with jewels and sparkly dresses under the lights. Some looked elegant, a few had tried too hard, but they all seemed to be having a good time.

She chatted with several of the older employees and noted names for future reference. Then later Bryn introduced her to a group who seemed to be genuine friends of his. They greeted her warmly but with curiosity in their eyes. She supposed they were wondering what had happened to Kinzi, but they were interesting and lively, and she began to relax, the smile that had made her jaw ache becoming real again.

Bryn left her briefly while he made a short welcome

speech and reminded everyone there would be an auction later in support of this year's good cause, the children's hospital.

When he rejoined her he said, "Duty done, now we can enjoy ourselves."

He swept her onto the dance floor, where a few people were either circling or swaying and moving their feet opposite each other. Bryn held her firmly with a hand on her waist and the other holding hers, and she effortlessly followed his lead. A number of young couples were dancing the same way. She recalled Pearl telling her that there had been a resurgence of interest after several TV programmes featured celebrities competing in ballroom dance.

Bryn said, "You like dancing?"

"Yes." She had always enjoyed it, had attended a jazz ballet class as a child, and before her first school ball had attended classes to learn the traditional waltz, foxtrot and some South American dances. "In America," she said, "I took up swing dancing for a while."

"With a partner?" Bryn deftly guided her past another couple.

"A friend," she answered briefly.

For a while they fell silent, their bodies in perfect unison while they moved about the floor. His hand on her waist brought her closer, her spine subtly bent to his will and their thighs brushing when he took another corner. Rachel's spirits began to lift into a dreamy euphoria.

As Pearl had predicted, the music from the live band was good, and Bryn was a great partner.

When the music stopped with a flourish from the drummer, Bryn swung her round in a circle, then caught her close for moment, smiling down at her before escorting her from the floor.

Her cheeks were flushed from the dance and from that brief contact with Bryn's hard, lean body. She was relieved when he noticed her empty wineglass and offered to get her another drink.

"Not wine," she said quickly. "Juice, please." She needed to keep a clear head. The combination of alcohol and spending half the evening with his arm about her and his mouth a tempting few inches away, their bodies touching for tantalising seconds as they danced, was likely to fog her brain and lead to unforeseen consequences.

Bryn wasn't drinking much, either. As the nominal host she supposed he, too, needed to take care.

When he excused himself for a couple of "duty dances" she got up with other men at the table, but they didn't have the same effect.

During the auction that created some exciting bidding for such things as an autographed All Black rugby shirt and an original drawing by a noted cartoonist, Bryn sat beside Rachel with his arm resting on the back of her chair. Earlier they had briefly inspected the goods on offer, and she'd lingered longingly over a papier-mâché box, small enough to fit on her palm, decorated with mother-of-pearl and lined with faded red velvet. Guessing it was Victorian, she'd assumed it would go for at least a few hundred dollars.

She didn't even realise that Bryn was bidding for the little Victorian box until the auctioneer lowered his hammer and called, "Sold to Mr Bryn Donovan! Thank you, sir."

"You bought it?" she said, turning to him in surprise. His signals must have been very discreet.

"You like it, don't you?"

"I do, but you didn't buy it for me?"

"Why not?" He shrugged. "All for a good cause. And there's nothing I particularly want."

"You can't—"

"Shh." He put a finger over her mouth and smiled into her eyes so that her insides turned to mush, before he returned his attention to the stage and the next item on the list.

On the way back to his apartment in a corporate taxi, they hardly spoke. Rachel was tired and yet on edge. The evening behind them had assumed a dreamlike quality.

Bryn at first seemed preoccupied, until he took her hand in his, raised it to his lips and said, "Thank you, Rachel. You were a delightful partner. I hope you weren't too bored."

For a moment she was too occupied with steadying her breath, her heartbeat, to reply. Then the effort to control her voice made her sound woodenly polite. "Of course not," she said. "I had a very nice time."

"Uh-huh," he said on a note of amusement that left her with no comeback. He didn't let go of her hand, holding it on the seat between them until they arrived at the apartment.

Once inside, he switched on the side lights, put a hand into his jacket pocket and drew out the papier-mâché box.

"Here." He took her hand again and placed the box on her palm. "A small thank-you for accompanying me tonight."

"There's no need, Bryn—"

"And for what you've done for my mother." He folded her fingers over the box.

"I'm being very well paid."

"Then look on it as a bonus, if you like."

She shook her head. It might be small but she knew what he'd paid for it. "I can't accept—"

"Rachel." As he had earlier he silenced her with a finger on her lips. "Shut up."

When he moved his finger she stubbornly tried again. "But—"

Bryn made an exasperated little sound in his throat, clasped her shoulders, bared where the lace wrap had slipped down her arms, and bent his head, giving her a hard, quick kiss that effectively robbed her of speech.

"Now will you be quiet?" he demanded, his voice deep and determined, his mouth, his eyes, inches from hers.

She blinked and hastily stepped back. "I'm going to bed," she said flatly, unnecessarily, making herself turn away. She knew he was watching her every step of the way until she closed the door of the room she was sharing with his mother.

Pearl was fast asleep in one of the twin beds.

Rachel went to the dressing table and lifted her hands to remove the pearl-and-diamond choker from her neck. Her fingers fumbled with the clasp but it wouldn't open. Turning it so she could see in the mirror how it was supposed to work didn't help. After five minutes she was still stumped.

She looked at Pearl, but all she could see was the blond curls on the pillow. It would be cruel to wake her. And sleeping with the necklace on didn't appeal.

Reluctantly she took the only alternative, returned the clasp to the back of her neck, left the room and knocked quietly on Bryn's bedroom door.

It opened almost immediately. His shirt was hanging loose, the buttons undone, but he wasn't yet undressed. She saw surprise flare in his eyes, and his lips curved. "Rachel," he said, stepping back as though inviting her in.

Quickly she said, "Sorry to disturb you, but I can't get this thing off," as she touched the choker.

Something flickered across his face, and then it became a wooden mask. "Okay," he said. "Turn around."

She felt him fiddling with the clasp, his fingers brushing her skin, then the small weight was lifted from her neck and she felt something else, the lingering warmth of Bryn's lips where the clasp had been.

She gasped, then turned to take the necklace from him.

He dropped it into her hand, and she parted her lips to say something—anything—but had no chance before his hands at her waist hauled her close and his mouth covered hers. The kiss was of such incredible finesse—a combination of absolute mastery and tender coaxing—that any thought of protest fled from her mind. She was too engrossed in the way his firm lips moved over hers, exploring their contours, and in the scent of his skin, the slide of his hands over her shoulders to her nape, tipping her head farther as his mouth urged hers to open for him, and a thumb settled on the leaping pulse at the base of her throat.

That small touch was unbelievably sexy, and she felt a hot shudder rush through her entire body, the sensation so exquisitely pleasurable that she made a sound like a brief whimper, her hands going involuntarily to his chest, bared by the open shirt, her palms flattened against the beat of his heart.

"What?" Bryn's voice was slurred as he lifted his mouth a fraction of an inch from hers. "Did I hurt you?"

"No," she murmured, barely above a whisper. Hazily she knew she ought to stop this, somehow, but the words wouldn't form on her lips.

He kissed her again, almost roughly, and she felt the scrape of incipient whiskers against her skin but it was more pleasure than pain. Then his mouth went from her lips to her throat and grazed along the line of her shoulder, and his arms brought her even closer as he kissed along the low neckline of her dress until she felt his lips on the curve of her breast.

The breath left her body in a sigh of sheer bliss, and he wrapped his arms about her, then raised his head to stare with glittering eyes into her face, his mouth taut and his cheekbones heated with dark colour. "Come to my bed," he muttered huskily. "I want you there *now*."

She knew he did—she could feel the arousal of his body, and her own was clamouring to do what he wanted, be what he wanted, wherever and as often as he wanted. Because she wanted him, too, with a fierce and almost overwhelming passion.

Almost.

Reason began a slow but inexorable return. She shifted in his arms, pushed ineffectually against his chest, until he got the message and loosened his hold although his arms still held her a few inches from him. "Rachel?" he queried, his eyes narrowing.

Slowly she shook her head. "I'm sorry. I shouldn't have let you... I should have stopped this earlier."

Bryn closed his eyes, and his head went back as he took a long breath through his nose, his mouth clamped tight. Then he abruptly dropped his arms and stepped back. "Your call," he acknowledged with a jerky nod.

He swung round and with a curt, "Good night, Rachel," closed the door on her.

Moments later she realised she was still clutching the necklace in her hand.

In the morning, when she came out of the guest room's en suite bathroom, Pearl was picking up the little box from the dressing table, where Rachel had left it.

"This is pretty," Pearl said. "Did you buy it at last night's auction?"

Rachel hesitated before reluctantly saying, "Bryn did."

"For you? Well, I'm glad to say my son has good taste."

"I can't take it," Rachel told her. "If you like it you'd better have it."

Pearl blinked at her. "It's only a trinket, Rachel."

Rachel stifled a laugh. "He paid a lot of money for it."

"I'm sure he could easily afford it. Even a Victorian lady would have accepted something like this from a gentleman friend without compromising her reputation. There's nothing *intimate* about it. If Bryn wanted to give you a present, don't hurt him by refusing it."

Rachel's eyes momentarily widened. Then she bit her lip. She'd thought he might be annoyed at her rejection of the gift, but even Bryn wasn't immune to ordinary human emotions.

Like hurt and pain—and passion.

How much of last night's unexpected passion had been for her, and how much a reaction to the pain of losing Kinzi?

Or simply a normal male response to a woman who had pulled out all the stops last night to make herself as alluring as possible, whom he'd danced with and smiled at and laughed with for hours, and who had probably been unable to hide her helpless yearning for him. And hadn't even tried to evade his kisses and caresses until he'd suggested the natural progression to his bed.

She grew hot again at the memory, and when Pearl replaced the box on the dressing table and turned, Rachel saw a flicker of surprise on her face, followed by a small, too-innocent smile before she headed to the bathroom.

Inwardly groaning, Rachel flung her overnight bag on her bed and dragged out a pair of jeans.

Over a late breakfast Pearl provided most of the conversation. Rachel didn't want to look at Bryn, after a quick glance had shown her an unsmiling expression that gave nothing away. But they both endeavoured to answer Pearl's questions about the ball and the people who had attended, and assure her they had enjoyed their evening.

Bryn asked if there was anything the women wanted to do or see while they were in Auckland, but after looking from him to Rachel, Pearl laughed and said, "After last night, I think you both need to relax today."

He gave his mother a keen look and said casually, "Okay. Why don't I fetch the Sunday paper, and after we've read it we can have a leisurely lunch before you two head home."

He turned to Rachel and offered, "Want to go for a walk, Rachel?"

Rachel politely declined. Whether he was going to ignore what had happened last night or conduct some kind of post mortem, she didn't want to know. His eyes when she met them were devoid of any emotion, and he shrugged, then left.

The three of them shared parts of the newspaper and the weekend magazine that came with it, swapping them around. Occasionally Pearl commented on some item, eliciting a response from one or both of the others.

It should have been a pleasant, companionable Sunday morning laze. Instead Rachel's nerves were stretching tighter and tighter. She hardly took in anything she read although her eyes moved across the lines, and every time Bryn shifted his feet or turned a page she felt the movement as if he'd reached out and touched her.

Ridiculous, she scolded herself. She knew he'd scarcely glanced at her, seeming absorbed in what he was reading, and when they'd all finished with the leisure section he began filling in the cryptic crossword.

After a while he paused, frowning over a clue, and then read it out, adding, "Any ideas?" Pearl laughed and said she could never work out what those things were about, she had enough trouble with a straight crossword.

Rachel said, "Landmarks."

Bryn gave her a look of respect. "Of course. What about this one?" He held the paper out to her. "Nine across."

Between them they finished the puzzle, and her tension gradually eased. But deep inside she smouldered with what she knew was unreasonable resentment after last night's torrid little episode. He was able to act as though it had never happened. That she was desperately trying to do the same didn't make her feel any more sanguine. Perhaps because Bryn seemed so much better at it.

He took them out to a late lunch, choosing an upmarket café near the harbour. They each had one glass of wine with the meal, and all the food came piled artistically on the plates into mini-towers that had to be dismantled before it could be eaten.

Afterwards they returned to the apartment and Bryn stowed the women's bags in the car before kissing his mother's cheek and telling Rachel, "Drive carefully."

On impulse Rachel said, "Actually, I'm a bit tired still, after the late night. Would you like to drive, Pearl?"

Bryn threw her a sharp glance and Pearl said quickly, "I…I haven't driven for ages. I don't think I could—"

"It's Sunday," Bryn said. "There isn't much traffic—it would be a good time to get back in practice. Do you have your licence with you?"

"Yes, in my bag, but…" Pearl paused, then said, "I had wine with lunch!"

Bryn's gaze turned quizzical. "So did Rachel. One small

glass, just like you did. Not enough to impair either of you behind the wheel. Is there some reason you shouldn't be driving? Something you haven't told me?"

"No." She seemed reluctant to admit it. "Not any more."

Bryn couldn't let it pass. "What exactly does that mean?" he asked. "If you were ill, why didn't you tell me?"

Pearl's surprise couldn't have been feigned. "I was never ill! Not really. The doctor said I'm very fit for my age."

"Then why did he tell me—" Bryn stopped himself there.

"What did he tell you?" Pearl demanded. Her blue eyes narrowed and for the first time ever, Rachel discerned a definite likeness between mother and son. "He had no right!"

"Nothing!" Bryn told her hastily. "He seemed concerned."

"Oh, for heaven's sake!" Pearl said. "I was feeling down after your father died—as anyone would! And very tired, just unable to motivate myself." Bryn nodded, obviously remembering.

"After six months I had a check-up, and there is nothing physically wrong. The doctor suggested antidepressants and I turned them down. I'm perfectly *fine*!"

Rachel let out a breath, sharing the relief she could see on Bryn's face before he frowned. "If he thought you needed medication—"

"I didn't," Pearl said stubbornly. "I got through it."

"In that case," Bryn said, "why aren't you driving?"

CHAPTER SIX

A GOOD QUESTION, Rachel thought, although wondering if Bryn was wise to push the issue. Perhaps she herself shouldn't have asked Pearl to drive, bringing the whole thing to a head.

Pearl cast her gaze about as if looking for an excuse, finally coming up with, "I don't like that car." Even to Rachel, who knew she still missed her red sports model, the excuse didn't sound convincing.

Bryn, too, looked sceptical. "You won't drive *any* car! Even when you're with Rachel you insist on her driving."

Pearl threw up her hands. "Oh, all right." Her cheeks flushed, she said, "I was caught speeding one time too many, not long before Malcolm…went. My licence was suspended for six months. And after that…I don't know," she finished lamely. "I just didn't want to drive. It had been too long and I suppose I'd lost my confidence."

Bryn stared at her, apparently baffled. "Did Dad know?" he asked. "About the suspension of your licence?"

His mother sighed. "I had to tell him in the end. Just before…it happened. The heart attack." Her voice wavered and her eyes filled with tears. "He was very…upset."

Bryn translated, "Angry."

Rachel moved to put her arm about Pearl's shoulders, giving him a warning look.

"What do you mean," he asked evenly, "*just* before he died? Minutes? Days?" Then, his voice gaining force, he said, "You're not *blaming* yourself for his death, are you? It could have happened at any time, the state his heart was in. It was just as well *he* wasn't driving when it happened."

"I know they told us that." Pearl wiped her eyes with her fingers. "But I can't help feeling…if we hadn't quarrelled the day before…we might have had more time."

Bryn stepped forward and took her hands in his. "Listen to me. If he was angry it was because he was worried. You *know* he loved you more than anything in the world."

"Oh, Bryn!" she protested weakly. "You and your sister—"

"He loved us, but he worshipped the ground you walk on."

A shaky smile briefly lit her face before Bryn went on. "He couldn't bear the thought of anything bad happening to you. And after that accident you had—"

"It was *nothing*!"

"It scared him. He wanted you to be safe, and happy. He never tried to stop you driving. If you'd told him you hate that car he'd have bought you another, so why don't you trade it in for something you like? But if I might make a suggestion, get one with a governor—or have one installed."

"A what?" Pearl queried.

Bryn patiently explained. "It limits the maximum speed."

"Oh. I suppose that would be a good idea."

Bryn exchanged a hopeful look with Rachel. Pearl might not sound exactly enthusiastic, but she wasn't dismissing the idea. She hadn't ruled out driving again.

He pulled Pearl forward a little, and Rachel let her protective arm drop. "Dad would hate for you to make your-self miserable over some kind of misplaced guilt," he said gently, looking into his mother's eyes. "No time like the present for getting back on the horse—or into the driver's seat."

Anticipating his raised glance, Rachel held out the car key, and he took it and placed it in Pearl's hand.

"Rachel will be with you," he said. "You trust her, don't you?"

"Of course I trust her." A hint of her old, pert smile curved Pearl's lip although her voice trembled a little. "Will she trust *me*?"

"Absolutely," Rachel assured her. Bryn seemed to be handling his mother's problem with insight and sensitivity and just the right amount of backbone-strengthening logic.

Pearl looked at the key in her hand, took a deep breath and said, "All right. Let's do it."

Bryn kissed her cheek. "Go for it," he teased, giving her a little push towards the driver's seat. "But take it easy, okay?"

Once seated, with Rachel on the passenger's side, she slid the key into the ignition, and took another big breath before turning it and carefully pressing the accelerator. The car moved forward slowly and after entering the flow of traffic Pearl's driving was unnaturally cautious. But by the time they'd crossed the harbour bridge Rachel saw that her white-knuckled grip on the steering wheel had loosened and her teeth were no longer fastened on her lower lip.

"She was fine," Rachel assured Bryn when he phoned that evening. Pearl was leafing through fashion magazines in the little sitting room and Rachel, deciding to make up for lost sleep the previous night, had been about to go upstairs when the hall phone rang as she passed it. "A bit nervous at first, but no problems."

"That's great." He sounded relieved. "You've been good for her, Rachel, getting her out of her shell."

"I like your mother. And I haven't really done anything except be around."

"Yes, and I appreciate that. Let me take you out to dinner one evening to show it."

"You've already treated me to a glamorous evening," Rachel said, after a moment's hesitation, "and an expensive present. There's no need—"

"That was business," he said. "And the present was for saving me from an awkward social situation and questions I didn't want to answer."

About Kinzi and the absence of a woman on his arm, he meant. Although Rachel was certain he knew other women who would have jumped at the chance.

Perhaps other women might have been less willing to accept the role of last-minute ring-in.

"Your mother bought me a beautiful dress," she said, "and you both refuse to let me pay for it."

"It was for a Donovan function. Would you have bought it otherwise?"

"No!" *Never in a million years.*

"I rest my case," he said. "Now, would one night this week suit you? Or you name a date."

As if her calendar might be full. "And your mother?"

"Do you feel you need a chaperon?"

"I thought you'd want to get her out, too."

"Let's not push her too fast."

"She'll be on her own."

"For a few hours. She's been on her own most of the

time for almost two years." His voice turned brisk. "I promise I'll get you home by midnight, Cinders. How about Thursday?"

She knew that tone. He wasn't going to give up, And further protest would seem like feminine coyness, which she despised. The stark truth was that the prospect of a night out with Bryn alone was alluring, even if fraught with hidden risks.

"All right," she said. "Do you want to talk to Pearl?"

"No need. I'll pick you up at seven on Thursday. There's a country restaurant I think you'll like, not too far from Rivermeadows."

Pearl seemed pleased when Rachel told her Bryn insisted on taking her to dinner, "As a reward for going to the ball with him, he said." She didn't want Pearl thinking it meant more.

On Thursday she dressed in a cool deep green sheath, a favourite that she always felt comfortable wearing on any occasion. Tying a gold mesh scarf about her hips, she wondered if that was overdoing it, but when she went downstairs and found Bryn already waiting for her, she saw he was dressed in dark trousers and a maroon silk shirt that even without a tie had a semi-formal look.

He gave her an approving once-over and Pearl assured her she looked very nice, and wished them a pleasant evening before they left the house.

The restaurant was almost an hour's drive away, attached to a boutique hotel perched on a hill giving spectacular views of native bush, with the city lights winking in the distance across an expanse of satinlike blue-black harbour.

The floor was carpeted and the tables covered in deep red damask with napkins arranged in fans at each place and fresh flowers in a low bowl on the table. Everything looked discreetly expensive. The dining room was arranged as a number of spaces holding only three or four tables and joined by wide archways, giving an illusion of intimacy, and easy-listening classical music played quietly in the background.

The maître d' recognised Bryn and led them to a table for two tucked into a lead-lighted bay window that overlooked the darkening landscape. A waiter appeared almost immediately with leather-covered menus and a wine list.

Rachel didn't ask if he'd brought Kinzi here. Almost certainly he had. Annoyed at herself, she studied the list in front of her and asked coolly, "What would you recommend?"

"They change the dishes often," Bryn told her. "The chef is a craftsman. I've never been disappointed."

When they'd made their choices he asked if she had any wine preferences, but Rachel shook her head and left that to him. He ordered wines by the glass, and after two he stopped drinking, saying, "You're not driving. If you'd like something else with dessert, or to finish with, feel free."

Rachel shook her head. As he'd promised, her scallops poached in white wine and the roast lamb that followed were delicious, and the crème brûlée she was now spooning up had been perfectly made with a crisp brown top. They'd talked about Pearl, and Rachel's research, and he'd told her about a timber-treatment company he'd recently picked up in America that had been a family business like Donovan's, then changed hands and went downhill.

"Simply through bad management," he said. "The buildings and plant are sound, though maintenance has been neglected. And they've lost some skilled staff, but with the right person in charge we can bring it back to profitability."

"How do you know when you've found the right one?"

"In the end it comes down to instinct and experience. I've not often been mistaken, but if they don't measure up to expectation, they're out of there with a handsome compensation package before they can do any more damage."

"Can you? Get rid of them just like that?"

"Sometimes the law makes getting rid of a useless, even dishonest employee harder than dissolving a marriage. But our contracts are fair, and I try to avoid legal wrangles."

"By paying them off?"

Bryn shrugged. "The price of my—or a manager's—bad judgement, hiring a dud in the first place. We all pay in some way for our mistakes. Money is the easiest."

"Money won't fix everything," she said.

"Most things," Bryn argued carelessly. "You'd be surprised how easy it is to sway people if you're prepared to part with enough cash."

The old Beatles song "Can't Buy Me Love" came into Rachel's head and haunted her for the rest of the evening.

When they reached Rivermeadows they entered by the front door. Bryn made sure it was locked behind them, saying, "Want a drink or something before we go up?"

"No, thanks." She hadn't known if he meant to stay tonight, but it made sense rather then driving all the way back to Auckland. Turning towards the stairs she said, "Thank you. It was as good as you said it would be."

"My pleasure." He began mounting the stairs beside her. "We should do it again some time."

When they reached the upper floor and her bedroom door he caught at her hand, bringing her to face him. "Rachel?"

His eyes were questioning, expectant, and something in her longed to give him the answer he wanted—perhaps anticipated. Her mouth drying, she made herself take a small step back. "Thank you again, Bryn," she said. "It was nice, although you didn't really owe me anything."

His lips curved, acknowledging the dismissal. "Any time," he said, not letting go of her hand. "Good night, Rachel." He bent forward and gently touched the corner of her mouth with his, lingering just long enough for her to change her mind and kiss him back.

She didn't, although inwardly wavered. When he stepped back and released her hand a pang of regret mingled with relief as she turned to enter her room.

In the following few weeks Bryn seemed to visit more often, sometimes appearing midweek and staying for the evening or even all night. Perhaps, Rachel thought, he was at a loose end with Kinzi gone, and hadn't yet found a replacement. Or was mourning her loss and not ready to involve himself in another relationship.

He'd developed a habit of giving Rachel, as well as his mother, a kiss on the cheek when arriving and leaving. Several times she went riding with him, and on the weekends that she'd gone to visit her family or old friends he commented that he'd missed her.

Sometimes he persuaded his mother to go out for lunch, both of them insisting that Rachel come along, too. Once while she was away in the Waikato he took Pearl to an outdoor concert in Auckland, apparently a great success. He was definitely coaxing his mother back into a more normal life. She had even invited some people over for Sunday brunch once after attending the little church in the village with Rachel. It had become a habit for Pearl to drive them there, but she still hadn't taken the car out on her own.

The day she announced to Bryn over breakfast that she meant to take his advice and buy a new car, Rachel thought for a moment he was going to stand up and cheer. But the glow of gladness in his eyes was extinguished by a certain caution as he said casually, "Good idea. I'll help you choose it if you give me a couple of days to clear some time."

"When I've found what I want," Pearl said firmly, "I'll call you and you can look it over."

Rachel could see Bryn wanted to argue, but instead he nodded. "Okay."

After he left, Pearl asked Rachel rather diffidently if she could take time off to look at cars in Auckland. Guessing she was still nervous of driving in the city alone, Rachel readily agreed.

It wasn't long before Pearl's eye was caught by a new-model silver Peugeot with dashing lines and a steep, raked-back windscreen. A test drive cemented her infatuation, and she asked the salesman to hold it until Bryn had time to confirm her choice.

He said if she liked she could take the car to Bryn for his approval. Hardly hesitating, with Rachel in the passenger seat, Pearl drove to the Donovan building.

Bryn's secretary told the two women someone else was with him, and they waited, flipping through magazines, Pearl impatiently tapping her foot on the carpeted floor.

When the door of his office opened he ushered out a tall, slim, thirty-ish woman, whose superbly cut and shaped blond hair framed an oval face, discreetly made up, and whose fitted skirt and short-sleeved jacket showed off smooth limbs and what Rachel suspected was a salon tan.

The woman held a leather briefcase in a ringless left hand while extending the other to Bryn and flashing him a smile that displayed white, even teeth. "I'll look forward to it," she said, their hands still clasped together. She—or was it Bryn?—seemed reluctant to let go. Even then, she touched his sleeve with her long, ringless fingers and gave him a quick peck on the cheek before turning to leave.

Despising the stab of envy that made her stomach sink, Rachel looked away. The long tanned legs and high-heeled pumps crossed her vision as the woman left and she heard Bryn's voice say, "Hello, Mother. And Rachel. Come along in."

"Who was that?" Pearl asked as soon as she was seated in his office, Rachel taking the chair beside hers while Bryn, as he had before, lounged against the desk, his arms folded.

"A client," he answered. "What have you two been up to?"

"We bought a car," Pearl told him. "Well, nearly. A Peugeot. It's in the car park, so you can look it over if you can spare a few minutes."

"We?" Bryn turned his gaze to Rachel.

Pearl said, "*I* did. Rachel helped."

"Hardly." Rachel shook her head. "I don't know a lot about cars, but your mother is comfortable with it, and it looks very…smart."

He looked with a pained expression from her to his mother and back again. "And I suppose that's important."

Rachel saw the crinkling skin about his eyes that warned he was teasing, and she said with dignity, "It's won awards for fuel-efficiency and it has lots of safety features."

"Are you in love with it, too?" he asked.

No, I'm in love with you! Much to her chagrin.

Of course she didn't voice the unbidden thought. "It's a very nice car. Pearl enjoys driving it."

He duly inspected his mother's acquisition, not saying

much but smiling at her enthusiasm, then took the salesman's number from the card Pearl handed him, flipped
open his cell phone and after asking a few questions said,
"Okay. If it's what you want…" Then he looked at his
watch. "Have you eaten?"

"Not since breakfast," Pearl told him.

"I'll take you both to lunch to celebrate."

Over salads and seafood, he asked, "What will you do
about the other car?"

When Pearl said she hadn't decided, he said, "You won't
get much for it, might as well keep it for Rachel's use."

"I can drive the station wagon," Rachel offered.

"It's harder to manage, and a gas-guzzler," Bryn said.
"You can go back to Rivermeadows together in the new
beast and I'll pick up the old one from the car yard and get
it back there to you sometime."

Apparently that closed the subject. Pearl simply nodded.
"Who was your client this morning? She's rather striking."

"Beautiful. And smart," Bryn said, causing Rachel
another pang. She'd never be able to compete with that
kind of svelte confidence coupled with physical perfection.

Bryn continued, "Her name is Samantha and she's Colin
Magnussen's daughter. She'd been running her own small
business in Australia and came home to take over the
family firm a couple of years ago, when he died."

"Magnussen?" Pearl repeated. "The builders?"

"That's right."

Even Rachel knew the Magnussen name. Ever since
she could remember, it had been associated with quality
public buildings and expensive homes. And the money the
family had made.

Samantha was one of the rich list, then. It accounted for

the surely expensive grooming and the air of privilege. There was no faking that. She and Bryn would have a lot in common; both had lost their fathers at a young age and had picked up the reins of the family's business.

Pearl said, "I met Mr Magnussen a couple of times at business functions with your father. A very opinionated man."

Bryn laughed. "Sam left the country and went out on her own because she couldn't work with him, although they were very fond of each other. He'd give her anything she asked for, but they both had very definite ideas about how to run the firm. She's doing a good job, though."

Obviously he admired Samantha Magnussen. For her mind? Rachel wondered hopefully. *Yeah, right.* The woman would make any man's blood run faster.

When they had finished eating Pearl went off to the ladies' room. Left alone with Rachel, Bryn said, "Are you getting your work done? You weren't hired as a chauffeur and lady's companion. Does my mother demand too much? Maybe we should be paying you more."

"The book is on track. And Pearl doesn't demand, she asks, and I'm happy to help. I don't want more money."

He laughed a little. "Then you're a rare being. Most people want all they can get."

Rachel looked at him curiously. Didn't his family have more than they'd ever need? Otherwise how could they afford to so generously support numerous charities and civic projects? Not that they trumpeted every donation to the world, but from the family papers she'd seen that generosity to the community was a Donovan tradition. The amounts they'd given away over the years staggered her. "Is that what motivates you?" she asked. "Making money?"

He seemed to think about it. "No," he said finally. "Not

directly. I suppose it's the satisfaction of adding to, building on, what my forebears began, the challenge of seeing how far we can go. And more urgently, of carrying on our industry in a way that helps maintain and heal the planet."

She hadn't realised he cared. "Sustainable forestry?"

He nodded. "Replanting, growing renewable timber, working with international entities to save rainforests that the world can't afford to lose. Getting products out there to make felling slow-growing, rarer trees unnecessary. Research into things like safer timber preservatives and even paints."

"So money is just a side effect?" she said slyly.

He laughed. "I like the competition of the market, get a buzz from being the best, producing the best. And that's expressed in terms of cold hard cash—or rather, figures in a computer."

"Big figures," Rachel murmured.

"Uh-huh. A measure of quality, and hard, honest work and good judgement."

Unlike his ancestor, Samuel, Bryn had never to her knowledge shoved a log of kauri or kahikatea or even the ubiquitous introduced pine onto a whirling saw to cut it into boards. And Rachel was certain he hadn't handled a ten-foot saw with another man to fell a giant of the forest. But in his own modern computerised world he worked hard, more brain than brawn.

Despite that he was as lean and muscled as any timber man of the nineteenth century. She was glad he hadn't, like those ancestors of his, grown a bushy beard to hide his lean cheeks and determined chin, and camouflage his beautiful masculine mouth. Just looking at him gave her a quiet delight.

Lately Bryn had treated her not very differently from the

way he had when she was the farm manager's brat from next door. Apart from the kiss on her cheek he bestowed at meeting and parting, he scarcely touched her.

He talked with her easily, occasionally laughed with her, shared music or a card game with her and Pearl during evenings at Rivermeadows, discussed the news or challenged her to Scrabble, or chess, which he played to win, sparing no quarter, yet was equally sanguine whether he won or lost.

She ought to be glad that he'd taken her at her word when she turned down his invitation to his bed. Glad that he'd backed off and offered no more sexy, difficult-to-resist kisses, that he apparently was able to forget those few minutes when she'd been nearly swept away by the power of his sexuality and her own weakness where he was concerned.

Many women would be happy to enjoy a casual fling with a man like him—even a one-night stand. Some might have regarded it as no more than a gesture of comfort to a friend, like a chocolate bar or a glass of wine.

But Rachel knew that for her, sex with Bryn on that basis simply wasn't an option. It would alter her life forever.

CHAPTER SEVEN

DAYS LATER BRYN and Rachel stood watching the Peugeot zip backwards out of the garage, turn smartly and head with a discreet roar for the road. "How could I have forgotten what gave my father his first grey hairs?" Bryn said.

"Oh, stop that!" Rachel scolded as they turned to his car, to drive to the riding centre. "Your mother's been driving longer than you have, and her problem with speeding has been solved. She's just a little quick on the accelerator and brake. And you should be grateful she's getting out and about again."

"Ganging up on me?" he grumbled. "My trouble is, I have too many women in my life. Even my secretary's been giving me advice about my…private life. I suspect she's been colluding with my mother."

That surely meant only one thing. Rachel tried to laugh, but something restricted the sound. She dreaded the day Bryn brought another woman to the house. A woman like Kinzi, or like Samantha Magnussen.

Dog in the manger, she admonished herself. That day was surely inevitable. She'd declined to share his bed, and once he got over Kinzi of course he'd find someone else. Not for a temporary balm to a wounded heart, but someone he could love and who would love him back with all her being.

As I would. If only he loved me that way.

Once they'd collected their horses Bryn set a pace too fast for conversation. On the way home they stopped again at the pub for coffee, talked across the table of inconsequentials, and she brought him up to date on the progress of the book, but they didn't touch on anything personal.

The following week Bryn treated Pearl and Rachel to a charity concert. Pearl insisted on lending Rachel the pearl choker again to add glamour to the new dress she'd bought to augment her wardrobe. Another simple style that would suit almost any occasion, it was a dark autumnal red with tiny glints of gold.

Bryn had said he would pick them up rather than having them drive into the city. When Rachel came downstairs to join Bryn and his mother he stood up and gave her a comprehensive, sweeping glance. His face was impassive, and maybe she imagined the quickly doused glow in his eyes before he said, "Very nice, Rachel. Shall we go?"

After the concert, featuring world-renowned New Zealand musicians and singers who held Rachel enthralled, they had supper at an exclusive restaurant with several people she now recognised from the newspapers or TV, even if she couldn't recall all of their places in Auckland arts and society. Bryn did nothing to satisfy the veiled curiosity in their eyes as they discreetly quizzed her. "I'm working for Pearl," she told them, after describing her profession and her present occupation. "And Bryn kindly invited me along with his mother."

Rachel was proud of her family and quietly pleased with her own accomplishments. Yet she was conscious that most of these people were either supremely talented or had been born to money, attended the most prestigious schools, expected the best in everything from food, clothes and entertainment to their homes and the yachts and motor cruisers that several of them owned and regularly sailed. Despite the egalitarianism deeply rooted in New Zealand's colonial history, the world they inhabited was subtly different from the one she had grown up in.

Rachel and Pearl stayed again in Bryn's guest room. In the morning he went off early to the office, and the two women browsed the city shops before enjoying a leisurely lunch in a department store café, and then visiting an art gallery where Pearl bought a small but pricey picture before they returned to the apartment.

There Pearl raided Bryn's drinks cabinet and poured red wine for them both, which in leisurely fashion they drank accompanied by a couple of cheeses Pearl had bought in a delicatessen, and some stuffed olives from Bryn's kitchen. The afternoon was well advanced when she announced she was going to have a nap. "Sorry to be such a bore, Rachel," she said. "I'm not used to late nights any more."

She was sleeping when Bryn arrived home, stripping off his suit jacket and pulling the tie from around his neck as soon as he entered.

Rachel had taken a book from his well-stocked shelves and was curled in a corner of the sofa with her legs tucked under her and her feet bare. Rashly, she'd poured herself another glass of wine and had been intermittently sipping it. Bryn was driving them home tonight and staying for the weekend.

"Hi," he said, eyeing her with an air of amused tolerance. "Don't move," he added as she made to close the book and shifted her legs, ready to get up. "You look very comfortable there." He ambled closer, tossing his discarded jacket and tie onto one of the chairs. Seeing the almost empty glass on the occasional table at her side, and spying the wine bottle, he cocked his head. "And helping yourself to my Ata Rangi Célèbre, I see."

Rachel flushed, stiffening. "Your mother's idea. She's having a nap."

"Hey!" The amusement vanished, his voice gently chiding. "You're welcome to the wine, and anything else you fancy." He turned her face with a hand cupping her chin, sending warm little signals along her nerve pathways. "Surely you know that."

His gaze met hers with perfect seriousness, and she tried to smile. "Thanks. I'm reading one of your books, too."

He smiled back, and removed his hand from her chin to lift the open book she'd dropped to her lap and check the title. It was a New Zealand historical novel by an author who regularly topped the local bestseller lists. "Like it?"

"Yes, she's good."

"Take it with you," he offered. He joined her on the sofa, his elbow resting on the back. He was sitting very close, and his eyes were grey and dark and strangely intent.

Rachel hastily dropped her gaze back to the book, but the words blurred before her eyes.

Bryn got up and lifted the bottle from the table. "Want to finish it?" he queried. There wasn't much left.

"No, I've had enough. Thank you."

He carried the bottle to the kitchen and came back with a half-full glass in his hand. Seating himself on the sofa again, he studied her thoughtfully.

Rachel closed the book, her finger holding the place. "How was your day?" she asked.

"Not bad." He sipped at his glass. "What did you do?"

She told him, adding that Pearl was fine though tired.

"And you?" he queried.

"I'm fine too. We had fun."

"Glad to hear it." His arm rested behind her head, and his fingers began absently playing with her hair, sending darts of sensation up and down her neck. "Don't you have a birthday coming up soon?"

"The fifteenth," she confirmed, not daring to move, although knowing she should. "Why?"

"We should do something special. Or are you planning on going home?"

"The weekend after," she said. "My mother's planned a family party."

He nodded. One finger was tracing a line up and down the side of her neck.

Rachel made an effort to keep breathing evenly. She ought to stop him, but pleasure was feathering down her spine, warming her entire body, no matter how she tried to ignore it.

"Bryn…" she said huskily.

His eyes were half-closed, lambent beneath the dark lashes. "Rachel," he returned, a hint of mockery in his tone, his mouth curving. His hand half circled her neck, bringing her closer as he leaned towards her, and his lips settled on hers.

It was a warm, tender kiss, their lips scarcely parted, and after a few seconds he withdrew, leaving her deliciously tingling all over, also surprised and disappointed.

It had hardly been more than a friendly peck but her head was spinning and her body felt weightless. The wine, maybe. "What was that for?" she asked baldly.

He laughed a little, and drank down some more of his wine. "Impulse," he said. "You're very lovely. Very kissable."

So was he, but she shoved that thought back where it belonged, in the deeper recesses of her brain.

"Do you mind?" His smile was a little crooked.

Wordlessly Rachel shook her head. How could she say she minded when it had been so nice, so…good. And what woman would object to being called lovely? But she said, "You can't go around kissing girls on a whim."

Bryn laughed. "I don't, usually. Only you." Then a strange expression crossed his face, as if he'd just said—or thought—something unexpected. "In fact," he said slowly, "I seem to have made rather a habit of it."

"Well, it's a habit you'd better break," Rachel suggested, but her voice lacked conviction—in fact she sounded to her own ears rather wistful.

"Do you really want me to?"

Rachel glared at him. "I'm not a rubber doll," she said, making him blink, "something you can pick up and put down when the mood takes you, a substitute for the real thing." She uncurled her legs and stood up.

Before she could take two steps Bryn had put down his glass with a thunk on the occasional table and was standing too, grabbing her arm. "Rachel!"

She tried to twist away, but he held her other arm, too, and she stood stiffly, not wanting an undignified struggle.

"Rachel," he said more quietly, "what's this all about? You think I was *using* you?" He gave her a small shake. "It's not like that. I couldn't resist, seeing you sitting there the way you did when you were a kid, but not a kid any more, the *realest* woman I know." A smile hovered on his mouth. "It just seemed right at the time. And you liked it, didn't you?"

"I didn't dislike it," she admitted. Strangely, she was sure that this time he'd been moved to kiss her for her own sake rather than because he missed Kinzi. "But the other times—" she said before cutting herself off.

Darn it, what was the point? She shrugged under his hands and he let her go.

"I can't apologise enough for that first time when you were only a teenager—"

"You already did, and I told you it's okay." It occurred to her that analysing every kiss they'd shared was a useless exercise. "Forget what I said. It was stupid."

"You always were a little firecracker," he said, a faint smile on his mouth, but his eyes were probing, curious. "Only I don't underst—"

Pearl's voice interrupted him from the doorway. "I thought I heard your voice," she told him, walking forward to give him a kiss on his cheek. "You're not quarrelling, are you?" She looked from him to Rachel, her expression a little worried, although her voice was light.

"No," Bryn assured her.

And Rachel said, "Of course not."

They exchanged a glance, both perfectly understanding that Pearl wasn't to be bothered by their private discord.

Back at Rivermeadows Bryn would have liked to continue their earlier conversation, but Rachel went straight upstairs and only came down to help with the dinner preparations.

After they'd eaten he suggested a walk around the grounds and a swim before bedtime, as the weather was warm now, but she declined, saying she was a bit tired, and avoided his eyes.

When he returned from his solitary stroll Pearl told him Rachel had gone up to her room.

"Is she all right?" he asked, taking a seat near the fireplace.

Pearl gave him an alert glance. "She told you she was tired. Is something going on between you two?"

"No." His answer was abrupt. Then he added, "But what if there was?"

His mother's eyes widened for a moment. "Why are you asking me? What happened this afternoon, before I interrupted?"

Bryn shrugged. "I told her she looked lovely. And kissed her. It was only a kiss—hardly even a real one. It barely lasted two seconds."

"And?"

"She didn't object, but afterwards she more or less accused me of using her."

Delicately arched eyebrows rose over Pearl's suddenly piercing blue eyes. "Would she have reason to think so?"

"No! At least—" Bryn rose, and paced away from her before turning. "It's complicated." He shoved his hands into his pockets.

Seeing he wasn't going to confide any more, Pearl said, "Rachel is a very nice girl, everything a man could want, and neither of us would like to see her hurt. So if you plan to kiss her again—or anything else—you had better be serious about her. Because if not you'll be answering to me."

Bryn frowned, meeting her stern gaze with a slightly glazed one of his own. Was he serious about Rachel? He'd never set out to "use" her. But at least once she'd had cause to assume so—when she'd been young and impressionable. And what else was she supposed to have thought now that ever since Kinzi and he had split, he could hardly keep his hands off her?

How could he persuade her otherwise—and make up to her for what he'd done, recently and way back when? That night still made him inwardly squirm with shame.

The answer was suddenly blindingly obvious. Focusing again on his mother, he gave a curt nod, unable to suppress a small smile at the unwonted severity on her pretty face. "You needn't worry," he said, the smile growing a fraction wider when she saw he wasn't going to add anything more, and her tightened lips metamorphosed into a frustrated pout.

The weekend before her birthday Bryn took Rachel to dinner at a club where they could dance. She agreed to go on condition he didn't give her a present, saying the Victorian box was more than enough. He sent her flowers—fragrant roses and lilies and baby's breath, delivered in the morning, with a card saying, "Love from Bryn."

She didn't take that too literally. It was an expression of a fondness he'd had for her since she'd been barely tall enough to reach his waist.

He returned her to Rivermeadows, kissed her cheek and then softly, her mouth, a fleeting caress, before saying, "Happy birthday, Rachel," and leaving.

When he asked her to accompany him again to a business dinner with a group of overseas clients, she said, "Why don't you ask your mother? She might enjoy it, now."

"She says she had enough business dinners when my Dad was alive, and she's old enough to retire from all that. If you help me out here, I promise to make up for it with a proper evening out another time."

"There's no need for that," she said. And that was enough for him to take her company for granted.

She wore the new red go-anywhere dress again and although much of the business talk was over her head, she supposed her role was to keep the partners happy, and played it as best she could. She'd insisted on driving in to Auckland, but agreed to stay at Bryn's flat afterwards with Pearl, who was happy to visit Auckland again and go shopping the next day.

The following weekend they had lunch at a nearby garden café before they went riding, and although Bryn's manner was casual, something in his eyes set off an absurd butterfly fluttering in her midriff and sent some kind of adrenalin rush through her veins.

Then it was a party he'd been invited to by friends. "You met them the night we went to the concert, and they liked you," Bryn told her. "I told them I'd bring you if I could."

"Do go, dear," Pearl said. "They're a nice young couple and I'm sure you'll have a good time."

She did, meeting equally nice new people while Bryn never left her side. This time they drove back to Rivermeadows in the early hours, Bryn having limited his consumption of alcohol while telling Rachel to feel free.

She'd had only one glass more than her usual limit of two, but felt pleasantly mellow by the time she arrived with Bryn at the door of her room. "Thank you," she said. "That was a good party. And your friends are fun."

"They hope to see more of you," he said, and took her face between his hands, making her heartbeat skip.

He smiled into her eyes, then his gaze settled on her mouth, and he kissed her, briefly and sweetly, as if just testing. Before she could even think about responding, he feathered a thumb across her slightly parted lips and then dropped his hands, stepping back. "Good night, Rachel," he said, and strode off to his own room.

Her only consolation was that she thought there was a slight unevenness in his voice before he turned away.

Rachel wasn't quite sure how it happened that they became a couple, but she soon came to realise Bryn's mother was aiding and abetting. Pearl's social life had become busy—visits, lunches and dinners with friends, invitations to other social functions, and her own hospitality to others now filled her calendar. She was frequently out of the house and when Bryn invited her along to some event she often pled tiredness or another engagement and said, "Take Rachel. She'll enjoy that."

Rachel did, and after demurring once or twice decided to go with the flow, make the most of her time with Bryn and try not to imagine a future without him.

One weekend they went sailing with a couple he knew and their baby daughter, a delightfully happy child just starting to walk. Everyone on board kept an eagle eye on the little girl, but she took a particular liking to Rachel, who found the feeling was mutual, returning cuddles with kisses and playing games with her when she got bored.

Her parents were quite open about her conception by in vitro fertilisation. "We'd tried for years," her mother told Rachel, "and in the end we were desperate."

The procedures she described sounded to Rachel invasive, undignified and sometimes painful, but both parents adored their daughter. Perhaps what they'd endured made her all the more precious.

Driving home, Bryn mentioned that his friend had confided in him during the difficult months of tests and procedures. "It was hard on both of them," he commented.

"She's a darling little girl."

"A pet," he agreed, "and I'm glad for them. Still, I'm damned if I'd allow a woman I loved to go through that. And there are no guarantees. If it fails it must be devastating."

"I suppose they knew that was possible but they felt it was worth it."

"Of course, but—" Bryn shook his head "—I'm not knocking their choice, but for myself, I'd never agree to it. Conceiving a baby in a Petri dish—well, I'm happy it works for some and I have to admire them for going through with it all. It's just not for me."

She could understand that. But they hadn't had the experience of wanting to have a baby and not being able to.

At the end of the day his good-night kiss lingered, and when he held her close she knew he was aroused, as she was. But apparently he was satisfied with kisses and didn't press her for more.

Satisfied? Not physically, she knew. But considering his seeming determination to keep their relationship on a near-platonic level, she could only think that he didn't want to get deeply involved.

Maybe the relationship between their two families was a factor. Complications could arise.

Or Bryn might be marking time until someone else turned up—someone who could unleash the passion she knew he was deliberately withholding.

The thought brought a sinking sensation in her stomach. She had begun to hope for the impossible—a future *with*

Bryn. Because wasn't this turning into an old-fashioned courtship? Or was she fooling herself?

Maybe he'd become accustomed to her being his stopgap partner, and didn't want her to get any ideas about permanence or real intimacy.

A flash of anger stopped the hot tears that threatened to spill. If he thought she'd happily put up with being at his beck and call when he needed a woman at his side, and fade into the background when he met someone classier, better-looking, from the same background, she'd...

What? she asked herself derisively. Make a jealous scene about it? The thought made her shudder. Ask him what his intentions were? Hardly better. He knew her time here was almost up. Perhaps he expected their...relationship—if that's what it was—to die a natural death when she left Rivermeadows. If he didn't commit himself in any way, what could be more convenient?

She had a draft of the book on her computer and was working on refining it, cutting, adding and improving, sometimes stopping to recheck a fact or time sequence. Bryn came on her one evening scowling over the screen in the smoking room, and bent from behind her typing chair to kiss her cheek. He gave her hair a tiny tug and whispered in her ear, "'Come into the garden, Maud?' It's a nice evening and there's a spectacular sunset out there."

Scowling even more fiercely because her instinct was to get up and blindly follow where he led, she said, "I'm busy."

Bryn straightened. Then he swivelled the chair around so she was facing him. "Hey, what's the matter?"

"Nothing's the matter. I'm being paid for this job and I can't drop what I'm doing every time you take a notion that you'd like company, or you need a woman on your arm for some corporate bun fight or society do."

"You *are* in a mood," he said, not in the least crushed. Folding his arms, he took a step back, nodding at the computer screen. "Isn't it going well?"

His tone was almost sympathetic, and that was nearly her undoing. The last thing she wanted was to weep on his shoulder. "It would," she said crossly, "if I wasn't interrupted. I only have a few weeks left to get the book printer-ready."

She swivelled the chair again and turned her back to him, staring at the screen without making any sense of the words on the white background.

His hands descended on her shoulders and began kneading the taut muscles. "Relax," he soothed. "No one's going to shoot you if you need more time to get it done. Seems to me you're working too damned hard and too long. It's way after five o'clock. Take a break and get some fresh air." He took her hand to pull her from the chair. "Come on."

Her resistance was short-lived. If only he'd snarled back at her instead of being patient and understanding, she'd have stuck to her guns. As he led her to the door she sighed sharply and said, "Sorry I snapped at you. I had no right."

"My hide's thick," he said, smiling at her crookedly. "And you have every right to tell me if I'm annoying you."

They stood on the terrace and watched the clouds strewn across the pale sky change from fiery red and molten gold to faded pink before turning grey and ghostly, and crickets began to sing in the creeping dusk. Bryn still held her hand and she let it stay, his strong fingers wrapped about hers.

"Let's walk," he said, and tugged her down the steps.

They walked under the archway and strolled beneath the trees that made the air cool and shadowed Bryn's face.

He stopped when they reached the summerhouse, with its festoons of faded jasmine and ivy geranium.

Rachel stiffened and tried to pull away, but he held her hand fast. "You're not frightened of me, are you?" he asked her. His face looked taut and his eyes very dark, a crease in the skin between them. "Not now?"

Rachel shook her head, a definite no. But her mouth was dry and she trembled. Why had he brought her here?

He took her other hand and said, "I scared you, that time. You said you forgave me, but I'll never forgive myself."

"I wasn't scared of you," she said. "I knew I could trust you."

Something crossed his face, like a cloud drifting over the moon. "That was your mistake."

Again she shook her head. "No mistake, Bryn."

He closed his eyes momentarily, squeezing them tight. When he opened them again they seemed brighter despite the deepening gloom all around. "Then you were a naive little fool," he said gratingly. "I was *drunk*. God knows what I'd have done if I hadn't had just enough sense left to send you away. Almost too late."

She had been naive, and foolish. He was right about that. And she was lucky that the man she'd chosen to throw herself at was Bryn. Even drunk he wasn't the type to take advantage of a stupid teenage girl with a serious crush on him and absolutely no experience of men.

She hadn't meant to incite him. Her impulse had been to comfort him in any way she could, and a hug seemed to be what he needed. And to kiss him gently was only natural. She'd daydreamed about kissing Bryn, but had never thought she'd have the nerve to actually do it. Nor the opportunity.

Or that he'd ever welcome it.

But that night was different. Bryn was hurting and she couldn't bear to see it.

He hadn't reacted at first to the kiss. She'd already been pulling away before he moved.

With her arms about him, she'd smelled beer and wrinkled her nose at that, but the hard strong body against hers, his arms coming around her, and another underlying scent she'd never smelt before, but that somehow thrilled her deep down, had woken new sensations.

Her breasts ached in a strangely pleasant way and she felt the centres tighten and harden; her breathing quickened and something shuddered through her like liquid fire, making every part of her—even the most private, intimate parts—feel sensitised.

Vaguely she knew what this was. Sexual arousal. She'd read about it, been told clinical, decidedly unromantic-sounding details in school, experienced odd, undefined stirrings. But nothing had prepared her for this—this overwhelming yearning to be closer, to know how it felt to really kiss a man, hold him, be held by him, let him touch her in places no one had touched her before that she could remember, in ways she'd only ever imagined or read about.

When he wrapped his arms about her, holding her so tight she could hardly breathe, and kissed her almost fiercely, opening her mouth irresistibly beneath his, she'd been both shocked and thrilled. She wound her arms about his neck, holding on to her balance, and tasted beer—and Bryn—in her mouth. She felt his hand on her nape, supporting her head, his fingers in her hair, and then he shifted to tuck her head into the crook of his arm, still kissing her in that desperately sexy way. He touched her breast, setting her on fire, so that she instinctively arched against him, going on tiptoe, her body a taut-stringed bow.

His pelvis thrust against her and she knew what she'd done to him. A flutter of alarm and disbelief mingled with a pagan, primitive triumph that must have been as old as time, when the first man and woman who had ever coupled discovered this marvellous, miraculous need for each other, this wondrous pleasure in each other's bodies.

Bryn lifted her, his hands at the top of her thighs, and staggered a little, then dropped clumsily to his knees so that she tumbled onto the sleeping bag he had spread on the ground and that earlier she'd tripped on. Then he was on her, touching her everywhere, his breathing harsh and heavy as he kissed her mouth, her neck, her shoulder, pulled at the neckline of her nightgown, then found the hem and shoved it upward past her thighs.

Since puberty she'd always been shy about her body, reluctant to wear a revealing bikini or throw off her clothes without thought in the school changing rooms. Now she felt exposed. A cold draught intruded into the summerhouse, sent goose-pimples up her arms and along her legs, making her shiver.

She looked up at Bryn's face and saw a stranger, shadowed eyes eerily blazing from deep sockets, cheekbones with the skin stretched across them, mouth set in a tight grimace. She felt the boards beneath the sleeping bag under her hips, shoulder blades and head. And the heaviness of the body that tangled with hers, all muscle and male strength. She had never known how strong a man's body could feel, that she would be helpless in a man's embrace.

Reality began to seep icily into her consciousness.

She tried to lift him a little, but he didn't seem to notice.

His hand stroked her inner thigh, down and then up, and touched the moist folds between them. The sensation was unlike anything she'd experienced, shooting through her entire body like a lightning bolt—a sharp, bright spear that brought part pleasure and part panic.

Panic and the sudden advent of shame won. She slammed her legs together and gasped, "No!"

Then she began to struggle.

Bryn reacted slowly, muttering, "What?" And when she repeated her repudiation, her voice high and alarmed, he said something explosive that made her wince. But to her relief he rolled over and off her, to lie panting on the bare boards.

"Get out," he said, his voice so thick and gravelly it was unrecognisable. He had one arm flung across his eyes.

"I'm sorry," she whispered. "I didn't mean—"

Gulping, she recalled her private vow not to throw away her virginity easily and early as some of her friends had done, often to their later regret. Romantically, she'd dreamed of retaining that gift that could only be given once, for the man she would love forever. And even in the throes of her immature crush on Bryn Donovan, she'd known in her heart that when she was truly grown up there would be someone else.

"I said," Bryn's voice came louder, harsher, "go! For God's sake—and yours."

Wretched, she stammered, "If…if I can do anything—" Boys said they'd be in pain if something like this happened. She swallowed hard, then leaned over to touch him. "I know you wanted—"

He swept her hand off. "I wanted a f— A woman," he said as if speaking through gritted teeth. "Not a bloody schoolgirl. Will you get...*the hell*...out of here before I do something we'll both regret!"

She gave a gulping sob and backed away, then turned and ran stumbling into the dark under the trees, oblivious of twigs snatching at her naked arms, unseen plants whipping at her legs and snagging the hem of her nightdress.

She lost a slipper, snatched it up and ran on with it in her hand; the shells on the path bit into her foot but she didn't care. Incongruously she thought of Cinderella, and even though tears poured down her cheeks she giggled, stifling the sound of hysteria by biting her teeth into her lower lip as she reached the open gate to home.

She had to stop and steady her breath before creeping across the back lawn and climbing through the window into her room, where she slipped under the covers and buried her head in the pillow so no one would hear her crying.

CHAPTER EIGHT

EVEN TEN YEARS LATER, standing at the entrance to the summerhouse with Bryn, the memory of that night had Rachel blinking away tears. She tried to shake them away, her hair falling about her face in the faint breeze as she moved. She pulled her hands from Bryn's clasp and dashed a knuckle against the corner of her eye where one tear had escaped. "I knew you would never hurt me," she said.

Except for that moment of panic when he'd seemed a frightening stranger, as though someone else had taken over his body. Until then the uncontrollable and bewildering physical need that had overpowered her own body made her more tense and nervous than anything Bryn had done.

Then he'd moved away from her, flung himself on his back and snarled at her to go. She knew now that he'd been trying to save her from herself—and him. "You did the right thing," she said. "If I hadn't been so young I'd have realised I was playing with fire. You wouldn't have had to shout at me to make me leave."

"I'm not sure exactly what I said," he admitted. "Only that it was pretty brutal. And you never gave me a chance to say sorry before you went south with your family.

Every time I tried to corner you, you scuttled away. I thought I'd terrified you, that you were afraid I'd attack you. Again."

"You didn't attack me! If anything, it was the other way round. I shouldn't have kissed you. It was stupid."

"It was very sweet," he said. "If only I'd left it at that…."

"Well, it doesn't matter now."

"It does to me. And I haven't been blind to the way you avoid this place. I want to…exorcise the ghost of that night, for both of us. Will you trust me, Rachel?"

"Yes," she said instantly.

He held out his hand and she put her own into it.

Bryn led her inside the little building, where a few fallen leaves whispered under their feet. The light was dim but not yet dark. He took her to the bench where they'd sat so long ago, and kept her hand in his as he sat and pulled her down at this side.

The trees outside cast faint moving shadows on the floor. A couple of curled, dry leaves scurried over the boards.

For several minutes they sat in silence, and gradually the tension she hadn't even registered began to leave her.

Bryn said quietly, "You used to come here often."

Rachel nodded.

"Before that night. And never since."

She didn't answer, but he knew. After a moment he said, "Me too. No one likes to be reminded of making an idiot of themselves. But lately I can't help remembering. And it isn't all about guilt and remorse, though I know it should be." He paused, and his voice lowered. "Does that disgust you?"

Rachel turned to face him. "No! It wasn't your fault I came here—"

"I'm not making excuses, Rachel. If I hadn't deliberately drunk myself out of my mind nothing would have happened. You know that. At least I hope you do."

Of course she knew. "If you brought me here to apologise again—"

"That's not why," he said. "Maybe it was a bad idea. I just thought—it's where we had our first kiss. And if you can discount how it ended… Can you? Or was the whole experience too horrible to think of?"

"It wasn't," she said. "None of it was horrible. But I wasn't ready for an adult sexual…encounter. If I hadn't stopped you I might have found it quite wonderful."

"I doubt it." His voice was clipped. "The circumstances weren't exactly ideal. *Was* your first 'encounter' wonderful? I hope so."

"They hardly ever are," she said carefully.

"I'm sorry," he said. "And I didn't mean to pry. I'd just as soon not know about the men you've made love to."

Of course not. Why would he be interested? She turned her head to stare out through the doorway.

He said, "If you can't stand being here…"

"No, it's all right. I'd forgotten how peaceful it always was, specially at night. Lovely." Tiny stars had begun to glimmer between the now stilled leaves of the trees outside. Other plants were almost indistinguishable in the creeping dusk, but she could smell their mingled aromas. Roses, jasmine, lilies. Perhaps more that she couldn't identify.

Breathing them in, she also breathed a different, closer scent, familiar yet exciting, unique to the man beside her. A combination of clothing and male skin, a hint of soap or perhaps aftershave, and something else—the subtle, alluring scent of Bryn himself.

She closed her eyes, every nerve alert. Bryn's hand

about hers tightened, and then his other hand was on her chin, turning her face to him, and she opened her eyes.

His face looked grave and taut, his eyes darkly glimmering. He fingered away a curling strand of hair from her cheek and tucked it behind her ear. His hand rested now on her neck, the thumb under her chin.

He lowered his head towards her and she didn't move. His mouth brushed hers lightly before he withdrew, studying her reaction.

Rachel swallowed, and her lips involuntarily parted a fraction, her eyes held by his.

He kissed her again, still lightly, though lingering longer, making delicious little forays before he lifted his head and said, "I hope bringing you here wasn't a mistake. That you'll have better memories after tonight."

Poignant ones, Rachel thought. If she let him kiss her again, that would be *her* mistake. Because if she kissed him back, and one thing led to another…

The thought of even one night spent making love with Bryn was far too enticing.

Maybe that was what he had in mind? To erase any negative feelings about this place—and about Bryn himself—by giving her a totally different experience, a gentle seduction as reparation for the past.

A sop, she thought bitterly. Not much different from the Band-Aid he'd insisted on applying after she'd stubbed her toe that first day of her return. Or the chocolate bar he'd given her when she was six and had scraped her knee and he'd taken her to his mother for some first aid.

If she succumbed to temptation now, she'd never get Bryn out of her system. She'd be crying inside for the rest of her life.

She pulled her hands from his and stood up, and he followed suit. "It was a nice thought, and I appreciate it. But if you brought me here to—" *have sex?* "—make love, thank you, but the answer is no."

"Rachel, wait!" She was almost at the door when he caught her hand again and made her face him.

"On a bare floor?" He shook his head. "No. I brought you here because I wanted to ask you to marry me."

She must be asleep—dreaming this whole thing. Her mouth opened but no sound came out. So of course it was a dream.

But surely her eyes were wide open? She blinked hard and widened them again. That seemed real enough. Bryn's hand on hers felt like solid flesh and bone and muscle. The sudden breeze that cooled her skin, and the rustle and plop of a possum dropping from one of the trees and scurrying over the fallen leaves, surely were real. And when Bryn grasped her shoulders and gave her a tiny shake, saying with a hint of laughter in his voice, "Is it such a shock?" the reality of it was unmistakable. "Rachel?" he said.

Finally she found her voice, although it came out in something resembling a squeak. "Yes."

"Yes, it's a shock, or yes you'll marry me?" he demanded. His hands tightened.

She almost said *Both*, but some dimly heard voice of doubt stopped her. "It's a shock," she said. "I had no idea—" *that he had marriage in mind.* "Why?" she blurted. "You're not...you don't love me!"

"Of course I love you! I've always loved you."

Not the way I meant. Not the way I love you, *as if no other man in the world exists for me, or ever will.*

"What do you think I've been doing these past couple

of months, taking you about, spending half my time at Rivermeadows?"

"Marking time," she said dazedly. "Until something—someone—better came along."

"You goose! It didn't take me long to realise I couldn't do better than the girl right under my nose, the girl I've known most of her life and a good chunk of mine. You're beautiful, and smart and kind and honest, and you make me laugh. If you say yes, Rachel, I'll be a very lucky man."

Wanting to fling herself into his arms, saying yes, yes, yes! Rachel reminded herself that if something seemed too good to be true it usually was.

Was this a rebound from his affair with Kinzi? Maybe he'd decided to play safe and settle for the less exciting, familiar girl next door after losing the glamorous, vivacious and high-profile Kinzi.

Bryn said huskily, "I love you, and I want you, as my wife and the mother of my children. You love Rivermeadows, don't you? We could live here and bring up another Donovan family, just as my mother wants."

His mother? Was this for Pearl's sake, because she made no bones about wanting grandchildren? Surely Bryn wouldn't allow her gentle pressure to influence him?

With a small, impatient sound, Bryn pulled her close, his hands going to her waist, and kissed her thoroughly, with skill and tenderness and increasing passion. And when her heart was pounding erratically and her body singing, he lifted his mouth and kissed her at the curve of neck and shoulder, while one hand slid to her breast, exploring the soft curve.

"You won't need to give up your career. I can afford all the help you need with the domestic side. Anything you want, it's yours."

He kissed her temple, and her cheek, and then her mouth again, this time quickly but firmly. He took her head in his hands and tipped her face. *"Anything,"* he reiterated.

She reached up and gripped his wrists, pulling away from him. It was impossible to think while he touched her.

"Rachel? Please say yes."

He stood rigid, waiting for her to answer.

He'd said he loved her. Asked her to marry him, have his babies. What more could she want? If his love was mostly affection left over from their earlier years, and only partly a new awareness of her as a woman, why complain?

Because if he couldn't give her his whole heart, perhaps he'd break hers.

But hers was ready to shatter anyway at the thought of leaving Rivermeadows, of cutting Bryn out of her life.

Either way she risked pain and grief. And if she took the coward's choice she would be turning down the chance of a lifetime—of spending her life at his side.

The chance to make Bryn really love her, and…

"Rachel?" His voice sounded raw, his body emanating tension even with a metre of space between them.

"Yes," she said. If she was dreaming, why spoil it? It was the best dream she'd had in years. "I'll marry you."

There, she'd committed herself.

For a long moment they stood looking at each other, though now she could scarcely make out Bryn's features in the darkness.

Then he stepped towards her and took her hands again, kissing them one by one almost solemnly, as if sealing her answer. "Thank you," he said. "I promise I'll do everything I can to make you happy. Shall we go and tell my mother the good news?"

* * *

If Rachel had held any doubts that Lady Donovan wouldn't approve, they were soon dispelled. Pearl was ecstatic, hugging and kissing them both, and insisting they telephone immediately to inform Bryn's sister over in England, and then Rachel's family. After that she took the phone and spoke at length to Rachel's mother about possible wedding plans, and on hanging up instructed Bryn to open a bottle of real champagne.

They finished the bottle before Pearl went up to bed, leaving Rachel and Bryn to follow.

On the stairs she stumbled a little, and Bryn laughed as he steadied her with an arm about her waist. "Can't hold your drink?" he teased.

"I'm not drunk," she protested unconvincingly. "Just a bit…happy."

He kissed the top of her head. "I hope you're a lot happy. I am."

At her bedroom door he gave her a quick, warm kiss on the lips, said good-night in a husky voice and gave her a little push inside. Then he left her, closing the door behind him.

Surprised but also relieved, Rachel readied herself for bed in a haze, partly due to the champagne. Maybe that was why Bryn hadn't suggested they share a bed—because she'd drunk enough to make her ever so slightly tipsy.

Once under the covers she began to go over what had happened in the summerhouse, reliving those wildly seductive kisses, and his astonishing proposal. Bryn had said he loved her. Maybe he wasn't *in* love with her, but that, according to the people who studied human behaviour, was a transitory condition anyway. In lasting relationships it gave way in time to a deeper and more enduring emotion.

Affection and some sexual attraction might be a better foundation for marriage.

All the same, she thought wistfully, it would be nice if they could share that once-in-a-lifetime experience that had inspired millions of poems, songs and love stories.

She couldn't help feeling just a little cheated.

Bryn presented her with a ring that had been passed down through the Donovan family for generations, but he slipped it on to her right middle finger. "I want to buy you an engagement ring," he said. "Until then, and afterwards, this makes you a Donovan bride." It was a wide band of gold, set with emeralds and a central diamond. He kept his hold on her hand and gently kissed her.

They were in the little sitting room, while Pearl busied herself in the kitchen after dinner.

Rachel looped her free arm about Bryn's neck and kissed him back almost fiercely.

As if taken by surprise, he drew away, then gave a quiet laugh and tugged her to the sofa, where he ensconced her on his knee and kissed her properly until she was breathless and flushed, and his eyes glittered with desire, his cheeks darkened. She was wearing a T-shirt and jeans, and his hand was inside the shirt, exploring the contours of her back, unhooking her bra, finding her breast with a cupped hand and running his thumb over the burgeoning centre.

Rachel gasped, arching in his arms, her head thrown back, and she felt his lips on her throat, burning a passage down to where the T-shirt's V-neck frustrated him.

He made a short, low and primitive sound, roughly pushing up the hem of the shirt, but quick footsteps in the passageway made him pause, and Rachel hastily scrambled off his knee to sit beside him, pulling the shirt down before Pearl entered the room.

She smiled knowingly at them, went to her usual chair and picked up the book that she'd left open on the arm. "I'll take this up to my room," she said, but instead of leaving right away she asked, "Have you two set a date for the wedding?"

"Not yet," Bryn replied. "But for me it can't be too soon. Is six weeks long enough for you mothers to make your arrangements?"

Rachel said, swallowing a nervous flutter in her throat, "Six weeks?"

Bryn turned to her, with raised brows.

Pearl repeated, "Six weeks! Is there a reason to hurry?" she asked, with a tinge of censure.

Bryn gave her a straight look. "Rachel starts lecturing in two months. I'd like to have time for a decent honeymoon."

"Need it be a big wedding?" Rachel asked tentatively.

"Not if you don't want it," Bryn said.

But Pearl looked disappointed. "It's the first Donovan wedding in a generation," she said. "Our relatives and friends will expect to be invited, and Rachel's family must have people they'd like to come."

Rachel supposed a Donovan wedding was always a lavish occasion. And she knew her own mother dreamed of seeing her only daughter married in traditional style with all the usual trimmings.

"Well," Pearl said briskly, "it'll be a stretch, but I daresay we can manage."

Six weeks later Rachel entered the little church at Donovan Falls on her father's arm, and saw Bryn waiting for her in front of the altar, his eyes dark and intent, his mouth unsmiling. He cast a comprehensive look over the filmy veil held by a wreath of white flowers, and the simply designed gown of brocaded satin featuring tiny seed pearls sewn into the fabric.

When his eyes returned to hers, he gave a small nod of approval, and as she neared him he held out his hand to take hers in his strong clasp.

The wedding ring he placed on her finger at the appropriate time was a plain gold band as she'd requested, and later she replaced above it the diamond solitaire in an intricate, finely wrought gold setting, that he'd bought for her days after his proposal.

In the last few weeks she had scarcely seen him. Apparently going off for a honeymoon meant he had various complex matters to take care of first. He hardly ever stayed at Rivermeadows and, when he did, he always said goodnight to Rachel at her bedroom door.

In the conscientious throes of finishing the manuscript of the Donovan history while consulting with her mother and Lady Donovan about the myriad details of the wedding, Rachel had her own reasons for being grateful that Bryn didn't press her for sex, yet couldn't help wondering at his circumspection.

Perhaps being in the same house with his mother inhibited him, although Pearl made a point of giving them time alone. Or maybe he just wasn't that impatient to take their lovemaking all the way.

When they went out it was with his friends. Bryn said he wanted her to get to know them. Rachel had lost touch with most of her friends in New Zealand, so not many of them were at the wedding.

The reception was held at Rivermeadows, and fortunately the weather was fine, although in case of rain a marquee was pitched on the front lawn.

Rachel fielded congratulations from all the guests and tried to remember their names. Among them she recognised the tall, elegant form of Samantha Magnussen wearing what had to be a designer suit and a wide, conspicuously stylish hot-pink hat.

"We haven't met," Samantha said warmly, smiling at Rachel after introducing herself. Apparently she hadn't noticed the two women waiting the day Rachel and Pearl had watched her leaving Bryn's office. "Bryn's a very good friend." Turning to him, she put a hand on his shoulder and kissed him on the mouth. Just a peck, then she stepped back, smiling again, her hand sliding down the front of his jacket before returning to her side. "Congratulations, darling. I never thought you'd do it. I guess even the tallest tree in the forest has to fall some time."

Bryn laughed. "Very philosophical." He hooked an arm about Rachel's waist and pulled her closer. "I'm a lucky man."

Samantha turned a coolly assessing glance on Rachel before her lips curved again. "You know," she said, "I'm sure you're right. Does she know what she's taking on?"

"I do," Rachel answered firmly. "I've known Bryn since I was five."

Samantha looked a little surprised but the smile didn't waver. "Well, I wish you all the best, and I hope you'll both be very happy." Her gaze shifted to Bryn before she strolled away.

Dying to ask Bryn just what that was all about, Rachel

had to turn to another well-wisher instead, and once the moment had gone there was no way of finding out without making an issue of it.

The day seemed to pass in a dream. Rachel kept reminding herself she was now Bryn's wife. He was by her side, his hand holding hers or guiding her through the throng of guests offering congratulations. Once the temporary tables were cleared from the big formal lounge room and they danced to the three-piece string ensemble, she felt she was floating off the ground.

When it was all over and she'd changed into street clothes, they drove off in Bryn's car to his apartment, where they were staying the night before flying to an exclusive lodge in the far north of the country.

After mentioning other people who had attended the reception, finally Rachel couldn't stop herself. Keeping her voice as casual as she could, she said, "Samantha Magnussen looked very elegant. I didn't realise you and she were close friends."

"Close?"

"That's the impression I had. Does she call all her friends 'darling'?"

A smile momentarily touched his mouth. "Probably. She's one of those women who just can't help using their femininity to advantage, but when it comes down to it, have steel at the core. In some ways she reminds me of my mother."

"Your mother?"

"It isn't a criticism. I love my mother, and I admire her hidden strength."

Rachel fell silent, and Bryn threw a quick glance at her as he slowed for an intersection. "You're not worried about Sam, are you?"

Sam? "Worried?" she asked innocently.

"Jealous." Bryn laughed in a rather pleased, indulgent way that made her hackles rise. "We're too much alike, she and I, both control freaks."

"I'm not jealous!" Rachel denied. She was sure Samantha wouldn't have rebuffed Bryn if he'd shown interest, but reminded herself he'd had plenty of opportunity and not taken it. Instead he'd been wooing Rachel, and it was Rachel he'd married. She'd hold on to that, banish Samantha Magnussen from her mind.

After parking the car they took the elevator to his flat, and he strode to his bedroom, dumped her overnight bag on a curved stool at the foot of the big bed and turned to her.

He seemed remote as his gaze took stock of her. "You look tired," he said.

Rachel tried to smile. She was deathly tired, the strain of the past weeks showing now the pressure was off. "I'm all right." Sounding overly bright, she knew.

She would have liked to walk into his arms, have him hold her, but he made no move and his aloof expression bothered her. Was he already regretting having married her, realising he'd committed himself to life with a woman for whom he felt only a lukewarm kind of love?

"It's late," he said, "And you've had a long day. My...*our* bathroom's there." He indicated the door. "Help yourself."

As if she were a guest. Rachel opened her bag, took out toiletries and the low-cut oyster satin gown she'd bought the previous week, and made her way into the bathroom.

When she returned Bryn was standing by the bed. He was barefoot and had taken off his shirt, loosened his belt. His hair was rather tousled, and he looked lean and handsome and very sexy. His eyes flicked over her and then away. "Finished?"

His voice sounded clipped. When Rachel nodded, he headed for the bathroom.

He'd turned down the bed covers, revealing pristine white sheets and pillowcases. Rachel hesitated and a picture flashed into her mind of Bryn and Kinzi lying there together.

Involuntarily she turned away, a hand at her mouth to stifle an anguished sound, and found herself at the window, staring at the closed curtains.

The room seemed stifling. She pulled back the curtains. There was no balcony, and through the glass she saw a few lights in nearby buildings, and the sky tower that dominated the cityscape of Auckland, lit with red and green floodlights.

She found a catch and pushed open a window, to be met by a roar of traffic noise from the street below, the wail of a police siren passing the building, and when that faded, the sound of music and voices coming from somewhere nearby.

"Hey." Bryn's voice startled her and she turned. "What are you doing?"

"I wanted some fresh air," she said.

"All you'll get there is petrol fumes and noise," he told her. He stood beside the bed, in wine-coloured pyjama bottoms that hung at his hips. They looked brand-new, still creased where they'd been folded. "I'll turn on the air conditioning."

He went to a control on the wall, and Rachel closed the window, but left the curtains a little apart.

Bryn had his hand on the light switch now. He said, "Get into bed."

She moved towards it, and paused. "Which side do you sleep on?" she asked.

His mouth took on a wry grin. "Mostly I sleep in the middle."

Mostly. When he was alone. Rachel took the nearest side, pulling up the sheet and blanket, her head on two pillows.

The light went out and she could see nothing for seconds, but she felt the mattress depress, heard the slight rustle of the sheet as Bryn lay down beside her. The bed was wide and they weren't touching. She could make out the shape of him now, in the bit of light that edged through the opening in the curtains.

He lay with his hands behind his head, apparently staring at the ceiling. Rachel made an effort to relax.

Bryn turned unexpectedly, his face a blur in the darkness, propping himself on one elbow. Rachel stiffened, her emotions a mixture of expectation and nervousness. There was something she should tell him before it was too late.

But with luck he might never know. Maybe she should just keep quiet.

His hand reached out and the back of his fingers touched her cheek in a brief caress. "Go to sleep, Rachel," he said, sounding rather weary himself. "You're exhausted. I'm not going to insist on consummating our marriage tonight."

Blankly she watched him slide down against the pillows again. Had he given her the real reason? Or…he didn't want to make love to her?

She wasn't the only one who was exhausted, she reminded herself. Bryn had been working hard so he could go on holiday without worries or interruptions. Now he'd closed his eyes and was breathing evenly, either asleep already or pretending to be.

Hardly the eager bridegroom she'd expected. She ought to be grateful for his consideration. Instead she felt flat, empty.

Rejected.

You know he wants you! she told herself. He'd said so,

and she'd enough evidence that he found her desirable. Men couldn't fake that as women might.

Desirable perhaps. But obviously not irresistible.

And on that lowering thought she went to sleep.

CHAPTER NINE

RACHEL WOKE TO the sound of the shower behind the closed bathroom door. When Bryn emerged, a towel tucked about his waist while he dried his hair with another, she was out of bed and rummaging in her bag for clothes.

"Good morning," he said, walking towards her, and as she straightened, her hands full, he dropped a kiss on her cheek. "We have an hour to get to the airport. I'll make coffee and toast while you get ready."

He had everything organised, and Rachel had hardly time to take a breath between leaving the apartment and getting on the plane. It was a small aircraft with only two rows of single seats, and within an hour they had touched down, to be picked up by a courtesy car from the lodge.

Surrounded by native bush and only a short pathway from the sea, the lodge was set in lawns and gardens. Built in Victorian style, with gables and a wide veranda set with a couple of outdoor tables, inside it was discreetly sumptuous.

Their spacious upstairs room, with its own balcony, had two queen beds and in one corner a two-seater sofa and matching armchair, with a round coffee table. There were tea- and coffee-making facilities and a well-stocked bar fridge, and they were given a choice of what they'd like for lunch, served either in their room or the dining room downstairs or, if they preferred, on the veranda with a view of the bay.

They opted for the veranda, and when their host had departed Rachel began unpacking. Bryn quickly did the same, and said, "We have time for a short swim before lunch. The lodge has a pool." From their room they could see a rough, white-speckled sea, with high, uneven breakers laden with seaweed and driftwood that were hurtled onto the beach and left behind by a vicious undertow. Although here the weather was calm, there must have been a storm out in the Pacific.

"Okay." Rachel picked out her swimsuit and hesitated, feeling stupidly shy. Bryn glanced at her with a tiny quirk at the corner of his mouth, and then turned away, beginning to unbutton his shirt. Rachel stripped and had pulled on the swimsuit before he turned around again, wearing shorts.

The pool was clear and sunlit, the temperature just warm. They swam side by side at first, then Rachel floated on her back for a while, contemplating the lazy, apparently unmoving clouds against an intensely blue sky. After a while she stroked for the pool edge and sat watching Bryn.

Eventually he breast-stroked over to her. Standing in waist-deep water, he gripped her waist in his hands and lifted her down.

Rachel gasped and involuntarily steadied herself with her hands on his bare, wet shoulders. He was giving her an oddly tight-lipped smile. "Now, wife—" he said. His head dipped, and his lips, moist and cool with water, found hers in a masterful, questing kiss.

Surprise held her motionless until his arms came about her, bringing their near-naked bodies into contact. Bryn coaxed her mouth open and a surge of joyous, delicious sensation made her shiver. Her arms slid around his neck, and he moved his hands down over the curves of her behind, then cupped and lifted her against him. His mouth travelled down the side of her neck, and nuzzled the soft flesh exposed by her low-cut swimsuit.

Her own response shocked her. She gave a cry as her body was consumed by pleasure, washing over her again and again, accompanied by a need to be closer to him, to experience this moment to the full, the ultimate physical delight. She was dimly aware that Bryn had shifted his stance, moving against her and prolonging the helpless, unstoppable spasms that seemed to go on and on, while she tried to bury her small screams and moans with her mouth against his shoulder.

As the paroxysm faded, she let out a long, uneven sigh, and heard Bryn make a guttural sound before his hold loosened and her feet again found the bottom of the pool.

She rested her bowed head against him, still tingling all over, not wanting to move and almost afraid of looking at him.

"Hey," he said softly. His cheek rubbed against her temple. "You okay?"

Rachel nodded, still not looking up, embarrassed at her loss of control. She moved her head up an inch or so and said, "What if someone had seen us?"

His chest shook with quiet laughter. "We're the only guests and the staff keeps well out of the way unless we want them. It's part of the deal. But we can continue this in our room. Where there are two perfectly good beds."

"It must be close to lunchtime."

And if they didn't turn up the staff would guess exactly why. Rachel moved away, and her eyes widened, a hand going to her throat. *"Oh!"* On Bryn's shoulder were the clear, reddened imprints of her teeth. "I'm sorry! I *bit* you."

Bryn squinted down at the marks, then laughed. "A real little tigress, aren't you? The scars of battle, which I'll wear with pride."

"No, you won't!" Rachel was horrified. "You'll put a shirt on. It's not a battle scar, it's a...a..."

"A love-bite," he finished for her. "All right, I'll cover it up if it embarrasses you." A glint came into his eyes. "But don't think you can make a habit of giving me orders, my sweet. I don't take kindly to them."

"Neither do I," Rachel informed him. The marriage ceremony they'd chosen didn't have any promise to obey. "It goes both ways."

He nodded, but she suspected he had reservations. They might have a few things to work out between them if this marriage was to be a success.

After leaving the pool and dressing they had a lunch of smoked salmon and salad with white wine before the staff disappeared, telling them there was a phone in their room and an intercom in the lobby, should they need any service.

Rachel sat staring at the hypnotic advance and retreat of the shallow waves washing on the curve of reddish sand that defined the little bay. A long way out a white sail dipped and swung on a faint breeze.

Bryn said, "Want to walk on the beach?"

"Yes." She got up quickly, discarding her sandals, and they walked across the buffalo grass that was springy underfoot, and onto the sand. It was gritty with the remains of the orange-red sandstone cliffs and the pulverised shells that had formed it.

Bryn put his arm about her waist as they strolled just above the waterline, defined by glistening clumps of sea-weed and a few stranded jellyfish, to an outcrop of smoothed grey rock that jutted into the sea and defined the bay. He had left his shoes behind, too, and when a rogue wave came in farther and deeper than the others, wetting his trousers, he rolled them up to below his knees.

He helped Rachel climb onto the rock shelf and they explored the tidal pools and watched the seaweed floating back and forth at the end, where the waves smashed against the rock and one sent spray flying into their faces and onto their clothes, making them hastily move farther back.

Rachel's cotton shirt and skirt were soaked with water that felt icy cold, and she tasted salt on her lips.

Bryn eyed her with interest. "You look like a contestant in a wet T-shirt contest," he told her.

Rachel made a face at him. "I suppose you're a regular patron at those."

A disconcerting gleam in his eyes, he said, "You'd win hands down." Then, "We could have our own private one."

His white T-shirt was wet, too. If there were male wet T-shirt contests he'd have her vote every time.

The sea breeze picked up, making her shiver, and Bryn said, "We'd better go and get you out of those things."

Back in their room Bryn stripped off his own shirt as soon as they were in the door, then strode to the bathroom and tossed it onto the marble counter before turning to Rachel.

The look in his eyes told her his intention, and her heart leapt as he grasped the edges of her still damp shirt and pulled it off when she automatically raised her arms.

He threw the shirt aside in the general direction of the bathroom, and looked at her, his mouth curving at the sight of the flimsy lace and satin bra. Rachel bit her lip and felt herself flushing.

His hands went to her waist, resting for a moment on

her skin, before he slid them around the top of her skirt until he found the zip at the back and it fell around her feet, revealing the minimal undergarment that matched the bra.

"Very nice," he said, his voice deeply approving. "But wet." His hands covered the bra, making her breath briefly halt. Then his thumbs brushed across the erect centres visible under the thin fabric, and he gently pinched them with thumbs and forefingers. Rachel closed her eyes and he said, "I'm not hurting you, am I?"

"No." Far from it.

Bryn lifted her face with both hands and momentarily she opened her eyes, to see his glittering with desire before his mouth descended on hers, sending her mindless with its erotic force and passion.

When he stopped kissing her he took her hand and swept the covers down on one of the beds, picked her up and lowered her to the sheet before shucking off the rest of his clothes.

"I've waited far too long for this," he said huskily as he came down beside her, leaning on one elbow. "But I'll try to take it slowly, for you."

He kissed her again, while his hand roved her body, and then he kissed her throat, the valley between her breasts, and her stomach, her thighs. "Sit up for a minute," he murmured and unhooked her bra, slid it off and pulled her back against him as he leaned on the headboard and began exploring her body with both hands, slipped a finger into her panties and made a small sound of satisfaction at what he found.

She knew she was about to explode again into ecstasy, and said, "No! Please…"

"You don't like it?" His questing finger stilled.

On a gasping little laugh she said, "I like it, but—oh, please, Bryn! I want you."

She heard him—felt him—draw in a breath. "I want you, too," he said. "But I want to see your face, all right?"

Rachel nodded. "Yes."

He manoeuvred her onto her back, and stripped off the flimsy remaining garment, then positioned himself over her, looking into her eyes before she felt him at the entrance to the most intimate part of her body, and she held her breath in anticipation, her hands on his shoulders. He muttered something and as he entered she briefly experienced an uncomfortable stinging sensation. She drew in a sharp breath, and he paused. "You okay?" he asked hoarsely.

"Yes," she breathed, "yes." And raised her hips, inviting him in. "I want you," she said again.

He felt so big, so hard and strong, yet as he moved slowly and gently her flesh parted around him, stretching to accommodate him, holding him snug within, and she started to relax as delicious little thrills ran through her, becoming stronger and more intense when he began moving rhythmically, looking down at her as if checking that she was all right with this.

And she was more than all right, her lips parting while the sensations gathered and spread and engulfed her so that she bucked against him and he released himself to her as the world spun and they were lost in each other.

He rolled over so she was lying along the length of his body, and with the movement she felt an aftershock of pleasure, rocking on him to savour and increase the feeling, while he held her close and whispered encouragement until she lay still and spent, her head dropped against his shoulder as her breathing steadied.

For a long time she didn't stir, and when she did Bryn still had his arms about her. They lay on their sides, face-to-face. He kissed her and said, "You're a wonder, Mrs Donovan."

"Really." *Better than Kinzi?* She pushed the thought away. Jealousy was destructive and unattractive.

He looked troubled. "Something felt…you were so tight. You're not…this can't have been your first time?"

Trying to sound casual, she answered, "Actually, it was." There was nothing to be ashamed of in sticking to a girl-hood vow, no matter that many people would have called it unrealistic.

His shadowy form remained still and the silence stretched. Finally he said, "Why didn't you tell me? I might have hurt you! *Did I?*"

Rachel shook her head, then realised he wouldn't see. "No. It was a little uncomfortable at first—"

He muttered, "I should have guessed."

"I thought maybe you had. When we were engaged, you didn't…you never suggested we should sleep together."

"It seemed the right thing, with you. Right to marry you, and…I hoped if I didn't press you for sex you wouldn't accuse me again of using you." His voice lowered. "And in a way it was a kind of penance."

"For what?"

"For the past." He paused, and in an almost stricken tone, asked, "Am I the reason you were the last twenty-seven-year-old virgin in the western world? What I did to you—"

"Don't flatter yourself," she said quickly. He seemed determined to cling to his sackcloth and ashes. Cutting down his ego was the only hope of stopping him. "Plenty of women have other things to expend their energy and emotions on. And it saves a lot of angst and complications."

"Hmph." He didn't sound convinced.

"Well, maybe it's harder for men," she conceded. "Although that's debatable. Historically in our culture they've been encouraged to think so, but social and cultural anthropologists have found—"

He laughed and hugged her closer. "I don't need a history lesson, my sweet." After a moment he said slowly, "I'm flattered you thought I was worth it."

Because I love you. She didn't say it aloud. He might have been perilously close to the truth when he asked if he was the reason she'd never slept with anyone else. Not because she'd been traumatised, maybe not even because of the romantic notion that she'd like to share something unique with the special man she hoped was in her future, but no other man had been able to match her memory of Bryn Donovan.

She was Bryn's wife. Even if he didn't feel as she did, he would keep his promises to love and cherish and be faithful to her. And being the man he was, he'd do his utmost to be faithful in heart as well as in body.

Shouldn't that be enough for any woman?

They made love every day, often several times, and at night, getting to know each other's bodies, exploring every plane and hollow and curve, every tiny imperfection, from the jagged scar Bryn carried at the top of his thigh from a childhood fall out of a tree, to the small round mole at the base of Rachel's spine that he said wasn't a blemish but a kissing spot, and set out to prove it.

They swam every day, too, in the sea after it had calmed and become benign and tame, teasing each other with games that turned to foreplay before they raced together, laughing, up to their room. At night they sometimes took a blanket down to the beach and spread it on the cool night sand in a hollowed-out cleft in the cliff, shadowed by plants clinging to its face, and made leisurely love there to the rhythm of the waves.

Bryn hired a car and they travelled to Paihia, where the first missionary settlement from England had been established, fighting an often losing moral battle with the whalers and traders who roistered in ramshackle inns across the water, and who stole girls from the mission with offers of calico dresses for themselves and firearms for their menfolk.

Once Bryn drove along country roads until they found an isolated spot where the thick bush held ancient kauri trees and hid outcrops of huge volcanic or limestone rocks. And on a soft mattress of moss beside a clear, stone-strewn stream, hidden among lacy ferns, he made love to Rachel in a way she would never forget. Afterwards they bathed naked in the stream, and Rachel came out aching from the cold water, but feeling more refreshed than she ever had before.

The time went by too fast, and the day came to return to real life, and Rivermeadows.

Rachel moved into Bryn's room, and persuaded Pearl that there was no need for her to find another home. "Later, maybe," she laughingly told her new mother-in-law. "When the house is full of children and you can't stand the noise."

"My grandchildren?" Pearl said. "I won't care how much noise they make!"

After Rachel began her new lectureship, she and Bryn often stayed in the city overnight, but she always felt that Rivermeadows was home.

The history of the Donovan family was launched at a

crowded, no-expense-spared function attended by local dignitaries and any employees or ex-employees who cared to come along, as well as some of Rachel's university colleagues. Pearl seemed in her element, presiding over it all and proudly introducing her son's wife to anyone who hadn't met her before.

After her first semester Rachel felt ready to cope with a pregnancy, but as time went on she became concerned.

Bryn said he was in no hurry but she couldn't help the nagging feeling that she was somehow at fault, not giving him what he'd expected from his marriage to her.

On the Internet she found all kinds of advice on diet and the things to avoid or to use to make conception likely, and took on board those that seemed to make sense. Certainly a lack of sex wasn't the problem. The opportunities now weren't as available as on their honeymoon, but it was still good, and she had begun to think that Bryn might even be falling in love with her.

Not that he was lavish with endearments or given to showering her with roses. But there was warmth in his gaze when it rested on her, lambent desire lurking in the depths of his eyes. He laughed often, and if business had parted them for a day or two his eyes seemed to light up when he saw her again. And his lovemaking when they were alone would be even more passionate and exciting than she remembered.

Pearl said, "Marriage suits Bryn. I haven't seen him so relaxed and happy for years."

On their first anniversary Bryn booked a table at an exclusive Auckland restaurant, and Rachel drove to the apartment to change into a new dress she'd bought for the occasion. Low-necked and figure-hugging, it was made of rich cream silk shot with amber.

She checked her clothes and make-up in the long dressing table mirror and picked up the pearl-and-diamond choker that Pearl had given her as a wedding present.

Bryn appeared behind her. "Close your eyes," he ordered, taking the necklace from her.

"Why?" But she did as he said.

Bryn's fingers were on her nape and her heart flipped. After a year he still had that effect on her.

Expecting the choker around her throat, she felt something cool and light and involuntarily opened her eyes, lifting a hand to touch the pendant that sparkled deep, deep amber with gold lights, on a delicately wrought gold necklace set with tiny diamonds. "Oh, Bryn!" she breathed. "It's beautiful!"

"I'm not done yet. It's part of a set." Her left hand was taken in his, and he slipped something over her wrist and fastened it.

She saw that the same unusual stone sparkling with more diamonds formed the case of the delicate watch, far too dainty for everyday wear.

Bryn said, "It's a nineteen-twenties cocktail watch. You don't mind that it's second-hand? I thought you'd rather like something with a history. Even though the shop couldn't tell me much about them."

"Mind? No!" He knew her well. "I love it—and the necklace. Thank you, but…"

She'd bought him a gift, too. Fossicking in a rare books shop during her research, she'd found an old map of the area around Donovan Falls and had it framed for him. He'd seemed pleased when she presented it to him earlier, but it cost a fraction of what he must have spent. She touched the necklace and said, "You must have paid an awful lot of—"

"Shh." He put his hands on her shoulders, meeting her eyes in the mirror. "It was worth every cent to see you wear them. Perfect with your eyes." He kissed her shoulder. "You look stunning. Ready to go?"

After a superb dinner, during which she intercepted several envious glances at the necklace and watch, they arrived back at the apartment and after shedding her shoes she went to the dressing table, placed the watch in the antique box he'd bought for her and raised her hands to remove the necklace.

"Don't," Bryn said, and came to stand behind her as he had earlier. He'd taken off his jacket and undone the top button of his white shirt.

Rachel dipped her head for him to undo the clasp of the necklace, but instead he wound his arms about her, pulling her close and kissing her nape, her shoulder. His fingers moved to the zip at the back of her dress and slowly slid it down, then he undid her bra, and slid both dress and bra down her arms.

"Bryn…" It was a feeble protest. His hands cupped her breasts and his eyes glittered.

She closed hers, and he said, "Don't be shy. Watch, darling."

Rachel opened her eyes, at first self-conscious, seeing her own body change under his ruthlessly erotic ministrations, the flush that spread over her skin, the way her breasts peaked between his finger and thumb.

Then she began to feel fascinated, excited, knowing that Bryn, too, was watching her every reaction, his breath like hers becoming uneven, louder.

When his roving fingers caressed her between her legs she gasped and writhed, then leaned against him, silently begging him not to stop. He didn't. Her head went back, her mouth falling open in ecstasy, and he gave a low laugh, pressing his own open mouth to the curve of her neck and shoulder, relentlessly bringing her to an orgasm that left her limp and spent.

She turned in his arms, burying her head on his shoulder until the last shudder left her body, and then he leaned forward, swept the tiny box, a comb, a hand mirror and a bottle of perfume to the back of the dressing table and lifted her to sit on it, before he stripped off his shirt and everything else and came into her while she gripped his shoulders and felt herself beginning to soar again, to that place where nothing mattered but this experience of mutual, uncontrolled pleasure given and received.

After a few moments he said, "Put your legs around me."

Rachel laughed breathlessly but did as he asked, and she laughed again when he lifted her again and staggered to the bed before collapsing on it, but the laughter died when another wave of pleasure unexpectedly washed over her and she had to cling to him, biting her lip and making tiny mewing sounds against the warm, damp skin of his shoulder.

"Go for it," he said, kissing her cheek, her ear, holding her tightly and gently rocking. "Enjoy yourself."

He was still hard inside her, and even as she went limp, dizzy and sated, he, too, came to another climax, holding her afterwards for a long time before they reluctantly parted.

When she finally fell into an exhausted sleep, her cheek resting on Bryn's chest, her last conscious thought was *Surely tonight we've made a baby.*

CHAPTER TEN

SHE WAS WRONG. Weeks rolled again into months, and still there was no sign of a Donovan heir. Pearl had begun to ask discreet questions, and although Rachel's own mother was reassuring, she had no magic fix. "It just takes some people longer," she said. "And if you're anxious about it, that only makes things worse."

Without telling anyone, in the long Christmas break Rachel asked the Donovan's doctor to refer her to a gynaecological specialist. Sometimes she had to pretend to be visiting friends or going off on an overnight research trip. After a long series of uncomfortable examinations and exhaustive tests she learned that her reproductive system had what the doctor called "congenital anomalies" further complicated by abdominal adhesions from the removal of an inflamed appendix when she was eleven years old.

"Surgery followed by IVF is possible, but the outcome is doubtful," he told her. "The chances of carrying a healthy baby to term are realistically…well, I'm afraid, almost certainly non-existent."

On leaving the doctor's rooms, distraught and shaking, her mind oddly blank, she walked for several minutes in the wrong direction before remembering she'd parked the car at the Donovan building, not knowing how long she'd be in town. In a daze, she turned and walked the several blocks back.

At the car she climbed in, then sat staring at nothing through the windscreen. Part of her wanted to go to Bryn's office, hurl herself into his arms and cry.

But some things even Bryn couldn't fix. She remembered his total rejection of artificial conception. Her own initial feeling was aversion to the whole concept.

She felt disfigured, ugly, as if anyone could see that inside she was what the doctor had called "malformed."

A surrogate? Their child in another woman's body? She wasn't even sure she could produce a normal ovum.

Yet if Bryn really wanted children of his own...

A baby that was Bryn's but not hers? Could she bring herself to accept that? Every instinct screamed no.

They could adopt, but surely what Bryn wanted was a child of his own flesh and blood to carry on the Donovan name and inheritance. To ultimately inherit the business, Rivermeadows, everything he and his forebears had built over time. Which she knew more about than he did himself after her delving into the family archives. There weren't many such dynasties in New Zealand, going back to pioneer days. It would be a tragedy if all of that were lost.

Absorbed in her thoughts, she didn't at first realise that the couple emerging from the office building were Samantha Magnussen and Bryn. Two tall, handsome people with the same air of confidence and success, walking in step with each other, Samantha's blonde head contrasting with Bryn's dark one that was turned towards her as she chatted to him.

Instinctively Rachel slid down in her seat, not wanting

them to see her until she could control her emotions. But she watched as they stopped by a car. Samantha unlocked the driver's door and Bryn leaned forward to open it for her.

Instead of getting in, Samantha turned to him, fingered a strand of hair back into its sleek style, tipping her head, and said something that made Bryn laugh. She laughed, too, looking up at him although he was only a few inches taller, and then he bent and kissed her cheek, and she gave his chest a casual little pat before she curled her long body gracefully into the car and waved as she drove off.

It doesn't mean anything, Rachel told herself. She might have fancied him but he married me. They're friends. Good friends. Though she'd never seen Samantha at Rivermeadows until the wedding, nor had Pearl known her before she and Rachel had seen her in Bryn's office.

Bryn was standing with his back to Rachel's car, seemingly looking in the direction Samantha had taken. Then he turned and strode to the building without looking around, and disappeared through the doorway.

Rachel took a deep breath. She could follow him, casually mention she'd seen him with Samantha.

And then?

Don't be stupid. The last thing he needed was a wife who didn't trust him.

Who couldn't even give him a child.

Bryn would never betray his marriage vows. Even if he were forced to admit he'd made a mistake.

Fear clutched her heart, creating a centre for the vortex of emotions that swirled inside her. Surely this news must make him rethink his commitment to her, to their marriage.

He wouldn't be underhanded about it—he'd be kind and sympathetic and generous—but wasn't continuing the family name his major reason for marrying? And if he wanted a divorce how could she refuse?

She turned the key in the ignition and drove out of the car park, not even sure where she was going until she had left the city and found herself on the road to Rivermeadows.

Halfway there she remembered she was supposed to be going to a business dinner tonight with Bryn, staying the night in the apartment.

Pulling over, she left a message with his secretary, telling the woman not to interrupt him, but "I feel a little sick. Nothing to worry about, only I don't think I can make dinner tonight. Tell him I'm sorry, and I'm on my way to Rivermeadows."

On her arrival she parked the car outside the garage and went in by the kitchen door. Pearl, coming to meet her on hearing the car, took one look, steered her to a chair in the kitchen and sat her down before brewing a cup of hot sweet tea and making her drink it.

When Rachel had finished it Pearl said, "Now tell me what's the matter. It isn't Bryn, is it? Have you quarrelled? That's normal in a marriage, you know. I'm sure it will blow over."

"No. We haven't quarrelled." Rachel had an urge to pour it all out to Pearl, but Bryn should be the first to know. Pearl, too, would be bitterly disappointed, and the longer Rachel delayed putting the devastating news into words, the better. "I'm a bit tired," she said. "And not feeling well."

She recognised the light of hopeful speculation in Pearl's eyes and said sharply in her anxiety to dispel the notion, "I'm not pregnant!" Her eyes stung and she turned away, hurriedly standing up. "If you don't mind I'll go and lie down for a while."

"Of course," Pearl said. "Can I do anything?"

Rachel shook her head. "I'll be all right." Her voice was muffled but steady.

With an effort of will she stemmed the tears before reaching her and Bryn's room and thankfully shutting the door. Then she let go for a few minutes before wiping her face with a tissue, then sat on the bed for a long time, knowing she must eventually break the news to Bryn. And Pearl. It was true she felt sick, nausea churning in her stomach. She rinsed her face in the bathroom, then lay down, trying to think.

What was she going to do? How was she going to tell Bryn? At least he'd be staying in the flat tonight after his business dinner. She'd have until morning...

She didn't remember drifting into an exhausted sleep, but was woken by the sound of the door opening. Daylight had dimmed, shadows filling the corners of the room.

"Sorry," Bryn said. "Did I wake you?" Then he was striding across the floor and taking her hands in his as she struggled to sit up.

He sat on the bed facing her, his face taut and concerned. "You're ill?"

"Not ill, not really. You didn't need to come. What about your dinner?"

He brushed that aside. "I cancelled. You didn't have an accident?"

"No." *Only an accident of birth.*

One hand touched her cheek. "You're pale. My mother said you looked dreadful when you arrived. Do you need a doctor?"

Her brain felt fuzzy. She must have been asleep for at least an hour, maybe more. This afternoon seemed like a nightmare, something that had never really happened.

"I have to tell you something," she said, her voice low.

"Okay, go ahead." When she didn't immediately do so he gave her a tight little smile. "I'm your husband, remember? In sickness and in health, for better or worse, etcetera. It can't be that bad."

She opened her mouth to blurt it out, then closed it again, reeling. *For better or worse…until death us do part.*

Earlier she'd reminded herself that Bryn would never break his marriage vows.

And suddenly she knew he would never ask her for a divorce.

All she had to do was tell him what she'd learned, or even say nothing and let the truth gradually sink in that they were not going to have a family. She could stay married to him, either way.

It was up to her.

She pulled her hands from his, sure she was going to be sick, and gasped, "I need the bathroom." He got up and she fled, a hand to her mouth, locked the door behind her and gagged emptily over the toilet.

"Rachel?" Bryn tried the door. "Are you all right?"

"Yes," she managed to say, finally finished. "Wait a minute."

She turned on the cold tap, drank some water, splashed her face again and dried it. Lowering the towel, she caught sight of her white cheeks and bloodless lips in the mirror, the faint blue shadows under her eyes.

Think. She needed to think. She had never deceived Bryn in her life. She couldn't imagine living with him and keeping her monstrous secret. Cheating him.

Staring into the mirror, she had a clear flashback of watching Bryn walking with Samantha Magnussen across the car park this afternoon, of realising how alike they were, both from the same kind of background, moving in the same world. So easy with each other. Samantha was the sort of woman who could no doubt run a large company with one hand and raise a perfect, healthy and well-behaved family with the other. The sort of woman a man like Bryn should have married. On first sight of her, Rachel had thought they were ideally suited.

Slowly she hung up the towel and opened the door. Bryn reached out to hold her arm and she flinched away. "Please don't touch me."

He frowned. "Are you OK? You'd better lie down again."

"I don't need to." She walked past him, then turned to face him, her hands clasped hard in front of her. He had his hands in his pockets, looking back at her with a baffled expression.

She said, "I…I'm so sorry, Bryn. The thing is, I want—" the last words came in a near-whisper, something clogging her throat "—to end our marriage. A divorce."

For several seconds he seemed turned to stone. Then he shook his head, his brows drawn together. "Divorce?" He stared as if she'd grown horns. "You can't mean that!"

"I do." She had to sound more certain. "I do!" she reiterated. "I made a mistake, a stupid mistake, marrying you. It wasn't right and I…" Her voice sank. "Please try to forgive me."

"What the hell are you talking about? What have I done?"

"Nothing! You've been wonderful."

"Then for God's sake…!" Apparently lost for words, he threw out a hand.

"I th-thought," she improvised, "that friendship and…and sex—" she swallowed "—was enough. We'd known each other forever, and I'd never met anyone else that...anyone I wanted to marry. It's a kind of loving, isn't it?" She couldn't help an ironic, sad laugh. "But not the sort to build a marriage on."

She was twisting the truth, attributing his motives to herself. "It's better to admit being wrong now rather than later."

Disbelief roughened his voice. "You really mean this?"

She could only nod. His expression was one she'd never seen on his face before—holding cold anger, disbelief...and suspicion. At last he said, "There's someone else." As if it were a proven fact.

About to deny it, Rachel hesitated. Would that convince him? She bowed her head, whispered again, "I'm sorry."

In two strides he reached her and gripped her shoulders. *"Who?"*

He looked terrifying, his eyes a dark, thundercloud grey, his face pale with the skin stretched over the bones, his mouth curled into something akin to a snarl.

"No one you know," she said. "Does it matter?"

His eyes narrowed. His fingers dug into her shoulders, and she knew he didn't realise it. In a strange way the small hurt was welcome, something that broke through the sense of unreality that surrounded her like an invisible cocoon.

"Tell me who it is!" he said. "His name."

"No!" But she needed to be more convincing than that. "He's someone I met at university. Another lecturer. But not in my department," she added hastily. If he could narrow the field Bryn might...

Might what? Once he got over the shock of her announcement, he'd calm down and be reasonable. Bryn was always reasonable. He had no real intention of tracking down her phantom lover. And if for some reason he tried, it would be a needle-in-a-haystack exercise.

His hands tightened further and she winced.

He released her, flexing his fingers. "How long have you known him?"

"Not as long as I've known you," she said, "obviously. But quite a while. I…we realised we're in love, and I tried, but I can't go on like this. I'll go somewhere else tonight, take the car if you don't mind, and some of my things. I'll get the car back to you."

"Keep it," he said.

"I can't do that."

He gave a harsh laugh. "But you can walk out on your marriage, just like that?" He snapped his fingers.

"Not like that," she said. "It isn't easy, Bryn, believe me. I don't want to hurt you—" Because he was hurt, she could see that. As any man would be whose wife said she preferred another. If nothing else it wounded his pride, threatened his masculinity. And she was certain Bryn had never thought that Rachel, who had adored him as a child, who had rashly offered him comfort as a teenager, and agreed to marry him as a woman despite knowing he felt little more than fondness for her, would let him down.

He'd get over it. And she…? She'd learn to live with what she'd done. Somehow.

She had to. "Please," she said softly, and she couldn't stop tears burning her eyes. "Please don't make it more difficult for me than it is, Bryn. I have to do this."

He seemed to be trying to see into her soul, with a burning gaze that seared her to the heart. "If that's what you want," he said at last, "you'd better go."

Rachel sagged, less with relief than despair. She'd burned her boats. "I'll…just pack a few things," she muttered. Banal words, the practicality of it seeming monstrously out of place when she had just destroyed the most important thing in her life.

Bryn didn't leave the room, but stood watching as she hauled a few undies and nightclothes from drawers and dumped them on the bed, picked up some other things from the dressing table. She crossed to the big rimu wardrobe and pulled out clothes at random, went back to the bed and only then thought about what she would put them in.

There was a small wheeled suitcase on top of the wardrobe, part of the luggage she'd brought to Rivermeadows. Dully she looked up at it, realising it was too high for her to reach.

Bryn, his mouth a straight, uncompromising line, walked over and brought it down for her, then flung it onto the bed.

"Thank you," she whispered, not daring to look at him. His silent fury seemed to thicken the air in the room, and she switched on the bedside lamp to dispel the gloom that filled it, and so she could see as she hastily stuffed clothing into the suitcase. Then she remembered she'd need shoes, and went back to grab a couple of pairs from the bottom of the wardrobe.

Bryn moved aside when she headed for the bathroom for some toiletries, and came back to add them before zipping the case shut. Automatically she looked around, checking if she should take anything else.

"Do you have money?" Bryn asked, as if the words were forced from him. "Your credit card?"

"In the car," she said. She hadn't even brought her shoulder bag in when she arrived, her single thought to get to

Rivermeadows and hide from the world. Not even a thought really but more of an instinct, like a rabbit pursued by a dog, running to the safe haven of its burrow.

Only it wasn't hers. Rivermeadows belonged to the Donovans and she would never again be welcome within its gracious, timeless homeliness.

She picked up the suitcase, finding it surprisingly heavy, and Bryn stepped forward, his face hard and cold and condemning. "Give me that," he said.

"I'm all right." A helpless longing engulfed her. Even now, he couldn't help his ingrained courtesy getting the better of him. She tried to resist, but when his fingers touched hers she relinquished the case. He held it easily, not immediately moving away.

"I'll see a lawyer," she said, trying to sound as if she knew what to do. "Unless you want to…"

"We'll both need one," he said harshly. "That's how it works. Let me know who yours is and mine will be in touch. It takes two years here, you know. No such thing as a quickie divorce."

She nodded. "Excuse me." He was blocking her way to the door.

He moved aside but she'd taken only a step when he caught her arm. "Goodbye, Rachel," he said. Then he dropped the suitcase, and his hand on her waist pulled her close. Her startled eyes caught a glimpse of his glittering, furious gaze, and the next instant he was kissing her with a raging, pitiless passion.

It took all her will-power to stay still and rigid in his arms. When his hold slackened a little she made an effort to free herself, but the kiss changed. His mouth became tender and coaxing, almost a plea for forgiveness, his hand cradling her head, his hold firm but no longer cutting off her breath, more as though he held something precious that needed to be handled with care, and knew his strength could break it.

He took her head in both his hands, his mouth still moving caressingly, beautifully over hers. She should push him away but was afraid to touch him, afraid that if she did, all her good intentions would fly out of the window and she'd be lost. She felt tears sting her eyes, sliding down over his fingers.

He lifted his mouth away from hers and looked at her, his thumbs stroking her wet cheeks. "Don't cry," he said quietly. His head bent again and he kissed the tears away. Rachel trembled, and raised her hands to his wrists, but tugging at them had no effect. "Bryn," she said. "I ca—"

"Shh." He cut off her feeble protest, and she tasted the salt of her tears on his lips as he claimed hers again, one hand sliding to her waist, the other cupping her nape.

No-o! her mind cried despairingly. But her body had never been able to withstand Bryn's lovemaking. She didn't resist when the kiss became deeper, and his hand found her breast. Her weak, "Please, Bryn," when he kissed her just above the V-neck of her top was hardly a convincing protest. Nor her momentary refusal to raise her arms when he stripped the top from her and kissed her again where her bra dipped in the middle.

By that time her blood was roaring through her veins and when they fell onto the bed together she already had her arms about his neck and had ceased to think at all. She was as eager to strip his clothes off his body as he was to remove hers.

They fell together into ecstasy, breast to breast, thigh to thigh, fused together so closely that his every movement was hers, her every sigh his, everything they felt when they reached the pinnacle of pleasure together was a part of both of them because they were no longer a man and woman but a single being.

Afterwards Bryn lay panting with Rachel's head on his shoulder. Slowly, behind closed eyes, her mind cleared and her heart turned into a cold, hard lump of lead.

Bryn drew a long breath, his chest lifting beneath her cheek, and he said, his voice low and certain, "You can't leave me now."

She wanted to stay within the loose circle of his arm, snuggled against him, never to move again. Reluctantly she began to edge away, but his hold tightened and he kissed her temple. "I'm damned sure you couldn't make love to me like that if you loved someone else."

"Bryn—"

"Don't spoil it," he said roughly. "Whatever the hell that was all about, it can wait."

She turned her head a little and kissed his skin. A reprieve, and she had a bittersweet few more minutes to lie in his arms and pretend everything was all right. But meantime she'd better decide what she was going to say when he demanded an explanation.

Maybe ten minutes later she realised Bryn was asleep. Another five, and she cautiously raised her head from its resting place and looked at him. The bedside light was still on, and he lay on his back, eyes closed and his lips slightly parted. Her heart turned over with love for him, and ached with sorrow. Carefully she edged away, lifted his encircling arm and lowered it to the bed before crawling out almost inch by inch.

She tiptoed to the bathroom and, afraid to turn on the

shower, gave herself a hasty all-over wash before quietly dressing again, retrieving the suitcase and opening the door.

She didn't completely close it before slipping down the stairs like a wraith. In the downstairs hall she paused. There was no sign of Pearl.

Glancing at her watch didn't help in the unlit hallway. Pearl was probably waiting with dinner, and keeping out of the way so as not to disturb her and Bryn.

Hesitating, Rachel saw the notepad on a polished table beside the hall telephone. She picked up the pen lying on top, biting her lip, then scribbled a quick note.

Almost silently she opened the front door, again leaving it slightly ajar, crept down the steps and stowed the suitcase in her car before taking off, her jaw so resolutely set that it ached, and the window wound down, letting the air flow inside, in an effort to stem the tears that stung her eyes.

CHAPTER ELEVEN

RACHEL STRETCHED and got up from her computer, made herself a snack in the kitchen of her flat in Dunedin, the country's southernmost city, and turned on her small-screen TV. She felt heavy and lazy, and when the doorbell shrilled it was a moment before she even realised that it was her bell and not the neighbour's.

Puzzled, she heaved herself from the chair and went to the door, hooking the security chain on before opening up and peeking through the gap.

Then she gasped. Her instinct was to slam the door shut, but Bryn stopped it with a hand on the panel and a foot on the step. "Let me in, Rachel. I'm not going away."

Her heart thumping, she considered for several seconds before giving in. But his stony, determined expression warned her he meant what he said, and she shut the door to remove the chain, then opened it again.

He stepped into the small hallway and Rachel backed to the room where the television was blaring through an advertisement for sporting goods. She crossed the room to switch it off before turning to Bryn, who was standing a couple of steps inside the doorway, staring at her, his face an odd waxen colour.

Automatically her hands went to her midriff, which only accentuated the visible bulge beneath the loose cotton dress she wore.

She saw Bryn's throat move as he swallowed, then he said, hoarsely, "Did the bastard leave you when he found out you were pregnant?"

Rachel's mouth fell open, and she blinked, then shook her head. "It's not like that."

"No?" He looked sceptical. "Why else did you run away, walk out on the university, move as far south as you could get? Did you know you were having his baby when you left me?"

"I didn't walk out—I told the university I had to leave." Pleading a medical condition, not entirely untrue, after she discovered that against all odds she was pregnant.

Bryn said, "I know your mystery lover isn't here. You live alone. What are you doing for money?"

The barrage of questions hit her like blows. She latched on to the last one, the easiest. "I have a job." She'd been lucky to be snapped up as a researcher by a local institute, and was able to do much of her work at home on the computer.

Bryn looked around disparagingly at the minimal furniture and slightly worn carpet that she'd dressed with a couple of cheap, colourful rugs. She hadn't spent much on her temporary home, thinking she'd need money later if…

There were a lot of ifs.

Bryn said, "Does he plan to do anything to help you—and pay maintenance for his child?" His voice was sharp, jagged. A coiled anger showed in his taut face in his eyes, which looked more deep-set than she remembered.

Rachel put a hand to her own eyes, her head drooping. She didn't know what to say to him, tired of the lie she'd been living, battered by his questions. Her knees were watery even though her legs seemed made of lead. "I don't need help. I can't—"

She felt his hand grip her elbow. "For God's sake, sit down," he said and led her to the sofa opposite the TV. He sounded more impatient than solicitous, and he didn't sit, looming over her with hands in his pockets and a scowl on his brow. "Do you want a glass of water or something?"

"No. Nothing." Particularly an angry man firing questions she couldn't answer. She looked up at him. "How did you find me?" Her phone number was unlisted; only her family knew her address and she'd made them promise to not divulge it to anyone, but particularly Bryn.

"Confidential," he replied. "Does it matter?"

Rachel supposed not. "Why did you come here?" she asked.

He didn't answer immediately. "My mother's worried about you," he said at last. "That note you left her didn't explain much. Sorry, thank you and goodbye?"

"Did you tell her…what I told you?"

"She was imagining all kinds of disasters, so I had to tell her in the end. She doesn't believe it."

But he had. Fortunately for her plan, yet that hurt more than anything.

Oh, what was the use of going on with this pretence? She looked away, staring blankly at the empty TV screen for a moment, then said, "She's right, Bryn. There was never any mystery lover. The baby's yours."

The stillness of his body, the silence in the room, were frightening. She didn't dare look up at his face.

From outside came the distant hum of traffic. Somewhere someone was playing rock music with a heavy beat.

Bryn's feet shifted, and he walked rapidly away. She squeezed her eyes shut, thinking he meant to leave.

But when she opened them he was regarding her from across the room. "What did you say?" he demanded, his eyes hard, chilling.

"It's true," she said.

"No." Bryn shook his head. "It makes no sense. You wouldn't have walked out on me—"

"I didn't know then that I was pregnant. In fact, it might have happened that day, when we—" She bit her lip. "The day I left."

"You expect me to believe that?"

"I hope…"

When she faltered, he said, "That I'd be mug enough to accept another man's child as mine? And keep you and… it…in the manner I stupidly accustomed you to?"

"You know me better than that!" The accusation stung unbearably. "I didn't ask—"

"I thought I knew you," he said. "I should have realised you'd changed, become a different person." He looked around again, taking in the less-than-luxurious surroundings, and frowned. "If you need money, I'll write you a cheque. How much do you want?"

"I don't want your money!" It was probably unwise to reject the offer. She might have to give up her job eventually. The specialist who kept an eagle eye on her had wanted her to stop earlier but she assured him the work wasn't strenuous and she'd be very, very careful. "My family will help if I need them to," she told him, hoping it never would become necessary.

Charity from Bryn wasn't an option after his monstrous accusation. Although she could hardly blame him for it.

"I didn't ask you to follow me," she said. "Why did you?" Not because of the baby, that had obviously been a shock.

He shrugged, but the movement was stiff, unconvincing. "We're still married," he said. "I feel some responsibility for you. When your bro— When I found out you were on your own, after all—"

"My *brother* told you?" Rachel's hands clenched. "I'll kill him! Which one?"

"Never mind which one. I practically had to tear out his fingernails to convince him it was in your best interests to tell me where you were and that you live alone. Your whole family is concerned about you. They didn't mention... that." He looked at her swollen stomach. "Do they know?"

"They will soon." She'd have to tell them. In the early stages of the split when she'd first fled they'd expressed shock, offered help, advice, frustrated that she'd say nothing about why she'd left Bryn. So far she'd managed to keep the baby secret, tried to convince them she was okay. Even when her mother flew down to Dunedin and stayed for a week. But if they came visiting now...

"My best interests?" she asked. He'd tracked her down and offered her money because of his overblown sense of responsibility, even though he thought she'd betrayed him in the worst way possible. "We're legally separated—you got the papers from my solicitor? You don't have any obligation to me."

He brushed that aside. "I won't have my wife living in squalor."

"Even though you don't believe the baby is yours? After accusing me of lying to get you—and your money—back? Now you've decided—what? Your pride or your reputation is in danger because I'm not living in a mansion? Make up your mind."

He scowled, running a hand through his hair. "It was a shock," he said, looking again at her body. "I hardly know what I'm saying any more—what to think. I *can't* see you in need, Rachel. We go back too far. You've become a part of me."

His final startling words went straight to her heart, bringing both pain and a small, flickering, feeble flame of hope. There was anger in his voice, his eyes, even in the colour that had returned to darken his lean cheeks, but underlying the anger was something else, something that sounded close to desperation.

Rachel swallowed hard, her eyes stinging. "You're a part of me, too," she said. "And—" she put her hand over her belly again "—so is this a part of you. I swear, Bryn, by everything I hold dear, this is your baby."

For the smallest sliver of a second she thought there was longing in his eyes but it quickly vanished. He looked down at her with hard scepticism, almost hostility. "It doesn't make sense. If that's true why didn't you tell me? You knew I wanted a family."

She had no choice now. "Because," she said slowly, "it was a miracle that I conceived at all, and—"

"Divine intervention? Congratulations."

She tried to ignore the sarcasm. "The day I left I'd just been told that my chances of having a baby were almost zero. I...I still might lose him—" she swallowed before going on "—though so far, thank God, he seems all right."

"He?"

"The scans say it's a boy. But...it might still turn out badly. A late miscarriage, or something wrong with the baby."

"That doesn't explain why you kept its—his—existence from me, if you weren't sleeping with someone else."

"There never was anyone else, Bryn. The only man I ever wanted was you. I lied, and I didn't come back when I found out the impossible had happened because I can't promise you a normal, healthy *live* child."

His eyes didn't leave hers, searching for the truth, and she didn't waver, praying he'd see it. She saw the scepticism, the unwillingness to be taken for a fool, fighting with other emotions—disbelief, anger, even grief.

When he spoke it seemed that anger had won. She heard it in the harshness of his voice. "And you decided not to tell me any of this? To spin some cock-and-bull story about falling for another man? What the *hell* were you thinking?"

She winced at his tone, but at least he might be starting to believe her. Without waiting for her reply he said, "I could shake you until your teeth rattle! What a damned *stupid*, brainless thing to do. And bloody insulting!"

"Insulting?" Rachel queried in a small, startled voice.

"Do you really think I'd not want my own son if he wasn't perfect? Or that I'd stop wanting you, *loving* you, if we couldn't have kids?"

"*I* couldn't. I thought you'd find someone else who could give you—"

"Well think again!" He strode over to her and pulled her to her feet. "I don't want someone else. Only you! Why do you think I married you? You're coming home to Rivermeadows with me, and I'm not letting you out of my sight until this baby is born, with the best specialists in the country looking after you."

"You could have a DNA test after he's born, if—"

"Oh, shut up!" Bryn growled. "I'd have taken you back even if the baby wasn't mine—so long as I had you."

"You wouldn't! You said—"

"Never mind what I said. The only thing I could think about all the way here was that I'd move heaven and earth to make you love me again and come back to me, because no matter how I tried to rationalise, convince myself you'd found a better man, that I was an obsessive, chauvinistic fool, deep inside I always knew you *belong* in my home, my bed, my heart. And in the end I had to at least try to make you see it, too."

Rachel stammered, "In your…heart?"

As if he hadn't heard, Bryn went on, his voice turning grim. "And then…I thought you were having *his* baby, and I wanted to kill him. I've never felt such a primitive, un-civilised emotion in my life."

"Are you saying—" Rachel hardly dared ask, but she had to "—that you're *in love* with me?"

Bryn glared at her, and for a moment she thought he might carry out his threat to shake her. "What sort of question is that?" he demanded. "Of course I'm in love with you! I told you the night I asked you to marry me—"

"That you loved me," she conceded. "But I guess you love my brothers, too, in a way, and—"

"I don't want to go to bed with your brothers!" Bryn drew in a breath. "How could you not *know*? From the moment you stepped off that bus and walked towards me, I was sunk, lost, gone!"

"Huh," she said. "It didn't stop you kissing Kinzi. And more, I suppose."

"All right," he conceded. It was the first time she'd ever seen him look even vaguely sheepish. "So I was a bit slow to realise what had happened to me. But I couldn't stop thinking about you, wanting to touch you, kiss you, be with you. And it was damned difficult to wait until after the wedding to bed you!"

"You didn't seem in a hurry even then."

"You were worn out and I wanted our first time together to be perfect for you. That night wasn't the right time. I shouldn't have rushed the wedding, but I was afraid I might lose you if I didn't get my ring on your finger before you were due to leave Rivermeadows."

Rachel shook her head. "I'd have waited for ever, for you. No other man would do."

"Is that true?" He scanned her face.

"Cross my heart and hope to die."

The old childish vow made him smile. Then he kissed her with great gentleness and great fervour, and said, "Let me take you home. Where you belong."

"Yes, please." Rachel sighed against his chest, already feeling that she had come home. Wherever Bryn was, that was where she belonged.

EPILOGUE

"HE'S PERFECT," Rachel said. Raymond Malcolm Donovan had been born by Caesarean section six weeks prematurely, because the specialists were worried that he'd outgrown his cosy but imperfect home.

He would be in an incubator for a while, but had been thoroughly checked at birth and had all the requisite fingers and toes and the right responses to stimuli.

Both his parents had been allowed to hold him for a few minutes, and now Bryn sat on the bed where Rachel was resting, holding her hand tightly in his.

"Clever girl," he said. "I suppose I have to forgive you for trying to keep him from me. I wouldn't miss this for the world."

"I'm sorry," she said. Now their time apart seemed like a bad dream.

Bryn would make a wonderful father. In the past couple of months he'd been nurturing her, protecting her, making sure she got the very best treatment and every comfort possible. His mother and her own family joked that he was besotted with her. But that was all right, because she was equally besotted with him.

"A Donovan heir," she said. "Your mother will be pleased."

"Over the moon. But I don't want you risking any more pregnancies. I couldn't bear it if I lost you. I waited ten years for you to grow up and come back to me."

She said, "You would have been disappointed if there were no children to carry on the Donovan legacy."

"We both would," he said, "but it wouldn't be the end of the world. I don't give a damn about the Donovan legacy, only about you."

"I thought I was second-best," she confessed. "After Kinzi."

"Idiot," he said, making the epithet sound like an endearment. "You—" he took her face in his hands and kissed her lightly, punctuating the rest of the sentence with more kisses "—will…never…be second-best…to anyone." The last kiss lingered, and she knew he was restraining himself, as if afraid of hurting her, until she slid her arms about him and kissed him back with fervour.

Then she drew away a little and said, "Not even your son?"

"Uh-uh. Not that I don't love him already. Until I saw him, he was an abstract, I'd have given him up in a heartbeat if you were in danger. But when I held him, something happened inside me that I can't describe. He's precious because you gave him to me. And I'll love you both until I die."

"I love you, too," she said simply. "And I'm sorry I was so stupid."

"Yes, well—when you're over this I'll be ensuring you make up for that," he threatened. "You have no idea what hell you put me through."

"Some," she said, remembering the dark, dreary days after she'd left him. And not at all worried about the kind of punishment he planned, knowing it would involve tenderness and passion and wonderful lovemaking.

Everything had come right in her world. Even though the future might hold unknown trials, they'd weather whatever life had in store, because they had each other. And right now, they were in their own heaven on earth.

HARLEQUIN *Presents*

International Billionaires

Life is a game of power and pleasure.
And these men play to win!

THE FRENCH TYCOON'S
PREGNANT MISTRESS
by *Abby Green*

As mistress to French tycoon Pascal Lévêque,
innocent Alana learns just how much pleasure can
be had in the bedroom. But now she's pregnant,
and Pascal vows he'll take her up the aisle!

Book #2814

Available April 2009

Eight volumes in all to collect!

REQUEST YOUR FREE BOOKS!

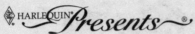

2 FREE NOVELS PLUS 2 FREE GIFTS!

YES! Please send me 2 FREE Harlequin Presents® novels and my 2 FREE gifts (gifts are worth about $10). After receiving them, if I don't wish to receive any more books, I can return the shipping statement marked "cancel". If I don't cancel, I will receive 6 brand-new novels every month and be billed just $4.05 per book in the U.S. or $4.74 per book in Canada, plus 25¢ shipping and handling per book and applicable taxes, if any*. That's a savings of close to 15% off the cover price! I understand that accepting the 2 free books and gifts places me under no obligation to buy anything. I can always return a shipment and cancel at any time. Even if I never buy another book, the two free books and gifts are mine to keep forever.

106 HDN ERRW   306 HDN ERRL

Name	(PLEASE PRINT)
Address	Apt. #
City	State/Prov. Zip/Postal Code

Signature (if under 18, a parent or guardian must sign)

Mail to the **Harlequin Reader Service:**
IN U.S.A.: P.O. Box 1867, Buffalo, NY 14240-1867
IN CANADA: P.O. Box 609, Fort Erie, Ontario L2A 5X3

Not valid to current subscribers of Harlequin Presents books.

Want to try two free books from another line?
Call 1-800-873-8635 or visit www.morefreebooks.com.

* Terms and prices subject to change without notice. N.Y. residents add applicable sales tax. Canadian residents will be charged applicable provincial taxes and GST. Offer not valid in Quebec. This offer is limited to one order per household. All orders subject to approval. Credit or debit balances in a customer's account(s) may be offset by any other outstanding balance owed by or to the customer. Please allow 4 to 6 weeks for delivery. Offer available while quantities last.

Your Privacy: Harlequin Books is committed to protecting your privacy. Our Privacy Policy is available online at www.eHarlequin.com or upon request from the Reader Service. From time to time we make our lists of customers available to reputable third parties who may have a product or service of interest to you. If you would prefer we not share your name and address, please check here. ☐

HP08R

The Inside Romance newsletter has a NEW look for the new year!

Same great content, brand-new look!

The Inside Romance newsletter is a FREE quarterly newsletter highlighting our upcoming series releases and promotions!

Click on the Inside Romance link on the front page of
www.eHarlequin.com or e-mail us at
insideromance@harlequin.ca to sign up
to receive your FREE newsletter today!

You can also subscribe by writing to us at: HARLEQUIN BOOKS
Attention: Customer Service Department
P.O. Box 9057, Buffalo, NY 14269-9057

Please allow 4-6 weeks for delivery of the first issue by mail.

IRNYNEW09